I0549212

MAVERICKS:
BAIT FOR THE LOBO PACK

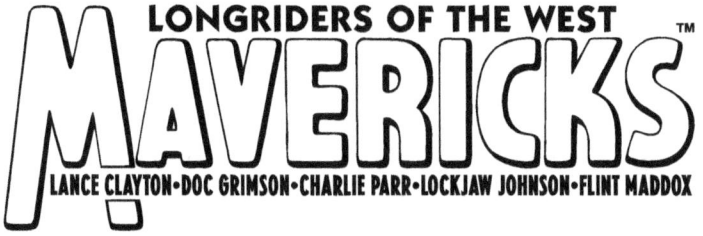

LONGRIDERS OF THE WEST
MAVERICKS ™

LANCE CLAYTON•DOC GRIMSON•CHARLIE PARR•LOCKJAW JOHNSON•FLINT MADDOX

BAIT FOR THE LOBO PACK

By Kent Thorn

POPULAR PUBLICATIONS • 2018

PUBLISHING HISTORY

"Bait for the Lobo Pack" originally appeared in the November 1934 issue of *Mavericks* magazine (Vol. 1, No. 3). Copyright 1934, 1961 by Popular Publications, Inc. All Rights Reserved.

ALL RIGHTS RESERVED

No part of this book may be reproduced or utilized in any form or by any means, electronic or mechanical, without permission in writing from the publisher.

CHAPTER 1
QUERIDA

LANCE CLAYTON'S eyes had begun to smolder. Charlie Parr stared resentfully, not with the indignation which had begun to boil in Lance's veins, but because he had a hunch that this trivial matter was about to interfere with their plans. Cold devils of humor danced in Doc Grimson's gaze because the same certainty had been on him for several minutes.

Flint Maddox felt his backbone grow cold. He had a profound aversion to cold steel, and this night was, for him, suddenly alive with knives. He had a feeling that they glinted from every shadow. He could hear the cold whisper of their flight in the little wandering swirls of breeze that came down from the Sierra Madre.

Lockjaw Johnson looked stolid. Foreseeing the course of events was not one of his weaknesses.

"About one more minute of that," Lance muttered, stiffening, "and I'm goin' to collect me a Mex scalp."

Charlie Parr raised weary eyebrows. "Better take it easy," he advised. "This thing we're settin' in is a tarantula nest. You're liable to git one in your pants if you start throwin' yourself around."

Flint Maddox let a brown, melancholy glance slide between them. "You're both right," he said. And added by way of fatalistic comment, "Damn it!"

Lockjaw Johnson straightened in his seat. "He's gittin' into your craw, Lance?" he asked, looking around him belligerently.

What his eyes fell on at first gave him no clew to Lance's irritation. Nobody along the bar, or at the tables bordering the *patio*, appeared to be paying them any special attention. The dark, Mexican eyes slid over them with the usual careful contempt for the "gringo dogs," but nobody was yet drunk enough

to want to start trouble with five gringos at once—particularly when all five of them were generously provided with heavy Colts and a distinct air of knowing how to use them.

All Mexico was in that long room—peons, with bare, dirty feet and tattered garments; strange, silent figures cloaked to the chin in blankets, eyes impassive under the big straw sombreros; dapper, slick-haired men in European clothes with pointed shoes; vaqueros from the neighboring ranches—hard, lithe, graceful—tricked out in tooled leather and clinking conchos. There were other men like them, yet somehow more swaggering, bolder, with the stamp of danger written on hard faces and a reckless, cruel expression upon mouths and eyes.

A room full of color, yet quieter than an American bar would have been. Movements were more careful, restrained. Voices and laughter were lower. The click of the roulette ball sounded clearly under the hum of the blurred, Mexican Spanish which filled the room.

To Lockjaw it was just another greaser bar. The fact that danger lived in it like a physical presence—that the five Americans were about as safe there as they would have been in a cage of half-cowed mountain lions—made no impression on him whatever. His horse-long, pugnacious face turned contemptuously from corner to corner. If anybody wanted to start anything…!

It was not until he had turned completely around that he came on the explanation of Lance's annoyance. One wall of the long room was broken in a series of wide arches which gave on an inner court. Their table, against one of these arches, gave a view of the reception hall of the *posada*, of which the bar was a part, across the *patio*. The hallway was wide and its full width opened onto the inner court. It was lighted, so that the white face of the girl and the heavy, ornately dressed figure of the Mexican who stood before her, arms folded and legs apart, were plainly visible.

Lockjaw's face registered comprehension and astonishment. "Hey!" he exclaimed protestingly—though whether he protested at sight of the Mexican talking to an American girl or at the inexplicable presence of the girl in that place, it was impossible to say.

THE ISOLATED village of Querido de la Sierra was about the last place one would have looked for an unescorted American girl who was also obviously a lady. Querida, the unofficial headquarters of that bandit known somewhat flamboyantly as the Wolf of the Mountain—*El Lobo del Monte*—was a town without law, unless it might be said that El Lobo himself was the law. A hard town, inhabited, if not by bandits, then at least by the relatives and friends of El Lobo's gang. So hard a town that even the Rurales avoided it, unless some specific duty sent them there. Then they went in force, and were not conspicuously successful.

Charlie Parr, to whom life had taught the caution and scepticism which Lance Clayton sometimes expressed and never acted on, viewed the girl with sour disapproval. She might, after all, not be the lady she appeared. In any case she was a nuisance and should have stayed where she belonged, instead of sticking her attractive and slightly turned-up nose into Querida and putting on the five Mavericks the obligation to protect her.

They had come to this remote section of Sonora on a difficult and dangerous adventure, the success of which depended on not incurring the hostility of either the town of Querida or of its ruler, El Lobo—at least until they themselves were ready to strike. In fact, if El Lobo were to suspect their business here more than their plans would be endangered; they would be lucky to get away with their lives. And the Mexican who at this moment was paying cavalier court to the girl, the man whose scalp Lance Clayton yearned to have, was El Lobo himself!

A vividly dressed Mexican at the bar watched the five at the table, reading their expressions. Then his eyes flashed across the *patio* to the figures of El Lobo and the girl. When he looked back at the Americans, there was a half-smile on his pock-marked face—a smile compounded of understanding, malice, and scornful amusement. He raised his eyebrows at three men standing at the other end of the room, making the downward gesture of the hand which in Mexico means "come here." They sauntered over and joined him at the bar.

They had barely gotten there when Lance Clayton gave a smothered exclamation of fury and got up from the table. El Lobo had reached down and taken the girl by the arm, pulling her toward him. Even across the court, the expression of anger and fear on her face was plain. It sent Lance out across the *patio* in long, swift strides.

Doc Grimson slipped, cat-like, out of his chair and followed.

"Keep an eye on the bar," he flung over his shoulder at the others.

By the time Lance reached the lighted entrance to the hall, the girl had been pulled, still struggling, to her feet. El Lobo, glimpsing the young American's approach out of the corner of his eye, turned a grinning face toward him. It did not occur to the bandit until he saw the blaze in Lance's eyes, that there could be anyone in Querida who would dare interfere with his amorous activities. He released the girl when he did see that blaze and turned to meet it with a sudden snarl. But the realization was a split second too late. Lance's fist, with a hundred and ninety pounds of steel-hard bone and muscle behind it, caught him square under the cheek bone and sent him hurtling across the room as though he had been kicked by a mule. He brought up heavily against the inn's small reception desk and for an instant lay there, dazed, the blood spurting from his cheek where the blow had laid it open.

A man had been leaning across the desk, chatting with the clerk. He was Pablo Bautista, El Lobo's lieutenant and bodyguard. The attack had taken him, too, by surprise. But only for an instant. As his chief struck the floor at his feet, his hand flashed to the scarf which circled his waist, came out with a throwing knife between thumb and forefinger. The blade flickered back over his shoulder, ready to shoot straight for Lance's unsuspecting throat.

The girl screamed once, sharply, as the throw began. There was the sudden blasting detonation of a Colt .45. A smacking flash split the air between Lance Clayton and El Lobo's slit-eyed aide. An instant later a metallic ring in a far corner told where the shattered blade had struck the tile-flagged floor.

The bandit's lieutenant was no longer slit-eyed. His lids were opened wide in astonishment and his jaw hung slack. He looked bewilderedly from the corner where lay what was left of his knife to Doc Grimson's slender, dark-clad form, outlined against the entrance, smoking six-gun in his hand.

Charlie Parr's voice rang out sharply from the dark outside. "Back! Or I'll blow the gizzards out of you!" The words were English and may have been incomprehensible to the four men who were racing across the courtyard, but the tone permitted no mistake.

The running footsteps stopped as the men brought up crouching. Then one of them made the mistake of going for his gun, trusting, no doubt, to the semi-darkness to cover him. One of Charlie's ancient and deadly hoglegs bellowed. The Mexican clapped his hands to his stomach with a sick grunt and went down. El Lobo had gotten to his feet, breathing hard—his black eyes full of the insane, hate of the Latin who has been struck with a fist.

Outside, guns began to etch the night with flame. Men were shooting from the bar, and the three who had been stopped by Charlie Parr's command had their guns out, shooting as they zigzagged back for shelter. Six Colts flashed and roared their answers as Flint, Charlie and Lockjaw thumbed deadly hammers in swift reply.

A MAN crouching behind the table that the Mavericks had just left gave a cry of pain and clutched at a shoulder blade smashed close to the neck. Another, by the bar flung up his hands and pitched forward on his face. One of the three outside gave down on one knee and then toppled sideways. A bullet from the bar ripped past Lance Clayton's shoulders just as several men with guns in their hands rushed the front door of the *posada*. Together Lance's and Doc's guns thundered, smashing the two oil lamps which lighted the hallway.

A blaze of orange flame leaped at them from the doorway as three men fired at once, but Lance had leaped aside, sweeping the girl with him, and Doc was flat on the floor, his guns chattering staccato pandemonium. There was one sharp yell of pain from the doorway and momentary silence.

"Outside, Lance!" Doc rolled out of the way as El Lobo's gun blared from the corner by the desk. Lance swept the girl into his left arm, whirled her through the doorway, and spun to a crouching halt against the wall. He waited a second until the fire from the bar momentarily stopped. "Now—with me! Run softly!" he whispered.

Holding her by the arm and waist, he rushed her to the shelter of the fountain in the center, praying that the noise of their running would not bring a hail of lead ripping at her slender body. But the Mexicans at the bar had been a little discouraged by the surprising accuracy of the American fire, which appeared to find the men behind the gun-flashes almost as shrewdly as it might have done by daylight. They had taken shelter and seemed in no great hurry to leave it. Several guns spoke, but apparently they were aimed blindly around the sides of pillars, for the shots went wide of any mark.

Charlie Parr materialized in the darkness beside Lance.

"No chance to get out front?" he asked in Lance's ear. His voice would have been inaudible two feet away.

"Blocked," Lance told him in the same murmur.

"Get her over the back wall then," he said briefly, "while we cover."

Lance waited a second and then, as the guns of the other three spat a screen of lead toward the bar, he raced with the girl to the wall. Once there he swung her high over his head. "Hold stiff!" he whispered and then shifted his grip so as to grasp her just above the knees.

The girl reached up, gripped the top of the wall, felt Lance's supporting grip under her feet and pulled herself up. "Lie flat," he whispered. Three swift paces took him to an iron bench which his memory told him was nearby. Lance set it lengthwise against the wall, so that its three metal arm-rests would serve as a ladder, and then crept back to pass the word to the others.

He found Charlie Parr first. "Work toward a bench about the middle of the wall," he murmured, then went in search of the others. Firing had become spasmodic, but his careful progress was too silent to attract attention. In a remarkably short time, he was back at the bench. He mounted carefully to where the girl lay stretched out on the wall.

"Let yourself down by your hands," he whispered. "I'll get hold of your wrist and lower you down."

The girl did as directed, wordlessly. Lance reflected with admiration that she had not once flinched, nor once spoken. When the soft impact of her drop told him that she was momentarily safe, he worked his way down the wall, away from the bench, let himself hang with his left arm over and his right hand holding a ready Colt. "Now!" he called in a clear sharp voice.

There was a soft rush of feet toward the wall, a second of silence, then a six-gun crashed from the reception hall. El Lobo had been quick to realize that Doc Grimson's besieging gun was no longer there.

Lance fanned two quick shots at the flashes, heard a sharp outcry of pain and fury, then turned his attention toward the bar, where other guns had begun to speak. Down the wall the quick scuffle of bodies and the sound of feet dropping to the ground told him that the others were over.

El Lobo's voice ripped through the darkness. *"Pronto! Han pasado el muro! After them!* Rouse the town! Death to the gringos! I, the Wolf, will make payment for their heads!"

The cry echoed from the bar, ran along the street outside, was taken up by voices throughout the town, *"A muerte los gringos! A muerte los cinco perros Americanos!"*—Death to the gringos! Death to the five American dogs!"

CHAPTER 2
MAVERICK NERVE

"NO CHANCE to get to our horses," Doc Grimson said swiftly. "Make for the edge of town and we'll lay up in the brush."

They set out on a run, Lance and Flint each holding one of

the girl's elbows, lifting her along to a faster pace. Someone shot at them from a window. A knife sizzled past, burying itself in the dust before them. Voices broke into cry behind them. They raced around corners, zigzagged through alleyways, but enough people saw them to direct the pursuit, and the rapidly growing crowd hung close on their trail.

They ran on, the girl breathing in gasps but making no other sound of complaint. For the short length of a side street no one appeared to see them. The houses were more scattered now. It looked as though they might make the brush, but realization was growing on them that, with the pursuit so close behind, they would have small chance to escape discovery.

They took the first side turn. From the iron-grilled balcony of the house next the corner came a gasping exclamation as a man got to his feet. He was holding a guitar in his hands and there was a girl beside him.

Lance Clayton pulled up sharply, his gun flashing out. "Put your hands up and don't move," he snapped in rapid Mexican.

The man above Lance raised his hands, one of them holding the guitar, with the quick movement of one who believes that death is not far from him.

From not far behind rose the cry, *"Por aqui! A muerte los gringos!* Here! Death to the gringos!"

"Get up there and fan him, Flint," Lance said quickly. "Lockjaw, give him a hand!"

"Good thinking, Lance!" Doc Grimson exclaimed in a low voice which had sudden hope in it.

Flint moved quickly, found the powerful stirrup of Lockjaw's hands, and sprang from it to the balcony. He fanned the Mexican swiftly for weapons, but found only a knife. By that time Lance was at his side.

He took the knife and held his gun in the man's ribs. "A sound out of either one of you and you die swiftly," he said in Mexican. Then to Flint: "Slip down and open the front door, so the last man can get in."

Charlie Parr swarmed nimbly over the railing, followed by Doc Grimson, who reached down to give the girl a lift up. "Get these two inside," Lance said to Doc and Charlie, "and tie and gag them."

"Take off your hat and coat," he told the American girl, at the same time shucking his gunbelts and tossing his own hat into the room. He followed it and emerged after a second with a Mexican straw sombrero on his head and a mantilla which he handed to the girl. "Cover your head with that," he directed swiftly, "so you hair doesn't show. If anybody speaks to you, keep your mouth closed and let me answer for you."

"Hablo Español com' una Mejicana," the girl said calmly.

Lance stared at her in astonishment. Below them, the front door closed softly after Lockjaw. "You speak Spanish like a Mexican!" he repeated scarcely able to believe his ears. *"Dios! What luck!"* His quick ear had assured him that this girl, like himself, spoke without the trace of an accent. But he had no time to marvel over this circumstance. The head of the pursuit reached the corner then, halted and hesitated as both streets showed empty before them.

"Eyah-h!" Lance yelled. *"Por aqui!* Here!"

The group turned and ran toward him. El Lobo led them. He was gasping and panting and Lance saw that his right sleeve was dark as thought blood had stained it. "Got him in the arm!" he thought, suppressing a grin.

"Is it six gringos you seek?" Lance asked eagerly. "One a woman?"

El Lobo paused under the balcony. *"Caramba!"* he panted. "God has given this one a brain of genius! Can you not hear, great dullard? Which way did they go."

"They took the turn of the next street, señor," Lance told him. "Running swiftly, the woman carried between them. I think they make for the open country."

"You think! You think! But you did nothing, eh?"

"Señor!" Lance's tone was pleading. "They carried many guns. I had not even my knife!"

But El Lobo had plunged on, cursing, and the crowd after him.

Lance sat down on the balcony and motioned to the girl to do likewise. "Would it not be better to go now quickly?" she asked softly, still in Spanish.

"Others will come," Lance replied, "and I think that soon now they will send back for horses, if they have not thought to do so already."

"Others must live in this house. If they should come…."

A MAN opened the window of a house diagonally across from them and stepped out on the balcony. He rubbed his eyes and peered sleepily across at Lance and the girl. The man looked as though he were about to call out to them, so Lance began to strum the guitar, playing one of the soft, keening songs of the hill country.

A group of men, variously armed and looking like people who had gotten hastily into whatever clothes were handy, turned the corner at a trot.

"*Qué pasa?*" demanded the man on the balcony.

"What little concerns thee," one of the group flung at him tartly. "Go back to your sleep, old one."

"Go with God, señor," the old man returned ironically. "On the way you may chance upon politeness."

Several of the group laughed and one stopped, with the air of a man who has run far enough. "Have you not heard?" he asked. "Five gringos have tried to murder El Lobo. All Querida is looking for them. El Lobo promises a donkey load of silver to him who shall come upon them first."

"*Aie!*" the man on the balcony exclaimed. "If I were they I would ride far and fast as though the devil was at my heels."

"That they cannot do," the man in the street told him, "for their horses are guarded. They are sure to be caught. It is said that one of them—a giant with flaming hair like the insignia of Hell itself—struck El Lobo such a blow as would have broken the neck of a lesser man. He will be flayed alive, when taken."

"And why was this thing?"

"Through jealousy of a gringo woman who looked on the Wolf with favor."

"*Aie! Las mujeres!* The women!"

Lance grinned through the darkness at the girl opposite him.

The man in the street passed on, and he began his strumming of the guitar again.

The man across the way stared at him, whether in resentment or suspicion he could not tell. He did not speak again.

"Where will you be safe?" Lance asked the girl softly, his voice mingling with the melody of the guitar. "Have you friends near here?"

"No," she told him swiftly. "I was going to a mine in the mountains—the Bar Bullion. My—the superintendent—was to meet me here. No one came."

"You started to say your fiancé?" Lance asked, the question slipping out before he knew it. He was conscious of the presence of Doc Grimson and Charlie Parr close within the dark frame of the window. They both understood Spanish and he thought he heard a small sound like a suppressed snort. His ears burned.

"No," the girl said calmly—perhaps too calmly. "I scarcely know Bart McAllister. I haven't seen him since I was a little girl. He is my superintendent. I am Doris Enderby. I own the Bar Bullion."

Lance stared and then suppressed an impulse to laugh. He could imagine Charlie Parr's face when he heard that! "You've played in plenty of luck, then—so far! Does El Lobo know you own the Bar Bullion?" he asked.

"I don't think so—why?"

"Because it's his private mine. Didn't you know he robbed two out of three shipments of bullion that came out of there?"

Doris Enderby gasped. "So he's the one! I knew there had been robberies, and the profits have sunk to almost nothing.

Bart—Mr. McAllister—wrote that he was having all kinds of trouble. The mine is my only source of income. I—I thought I had better come and see."

Lance saw the shutters across the way move ever so little and knew that the old man was watching through them. A beat of horses' hoofs sounded from the center of town, growing in volume. He knew that they would have to wait until the horses passed, but something told him that they had better get out of there, and soon as possible.

"I—I'm afraid you've gotten yourselves into terrible trouble on my account," the girl said. "Do you live here, or are you just on your way somewhere?"

"Er—just kind of passing through." It would hardly do to tell this girl that they had come here to rob her mine! Or rather, that they intended to relieve El Lobo of his next booty after he had gotten it, which would come to the same thing from her point of view—though not from theirs.

Word had filtered down to the Border towns that El Lobo was levying regular toll on the Bar Bullion mine—getting rich at it. It had brought the five Mavericks riding into the heart of Sonora, because swooping down on the bandit chief and his gang was a job cut exactly to the order of their brand of outlawry. In order to accomplish it, they had to ride more than two hundred miles into unfriendly territory, make their investigations in the Wolf's den itself, strike swiftly and skilfully and manage to re-traverse those hot, hostile desert miles, handicapped by a donkey train burdened with silver bullion!

It was the kind of exploit for which the quintette had made

itself famous from the Badlands of Montana to the hills of Chihuahua. Known unfavorably to the law, they were equally unpopular with certain riders of the Owlhoot Trail. But if certain brands of outlaws had reason to curse them equally with a number of lawmen, many an honest unfortunate rancher and cow-poke had had reason to swear by them, and did.

CHARLEY PARR, white-mustached whose keen, ageless blue eyes were set in a mass of wrinkles, was an old-timer on the Owlhoot Trail. He had been a member of Boot Hill Kennedy's famous gang until he and Kennedy had disagreed about the promiscuous killing of innocent bystanders. The ensuing argument had resulted fatally to Boot Hill and for a short time Charlie had led the gang, until finally, finding himself at odds with the men under him, he had hit the trail alone, except for the faithful Lockjaw Johnson, whose loyalty was of the kind which asks no questions and has no reservations.

Flint Maddox, once a respectable ranch-owner, had been ruined by a neighboring land-hog, his wife and children being lost in an incendiary fire, for which Flint had reason to believe his enemy had been responsible. He had killed the ranchman and his foreman in a saloon fight, and had been forced outside the law by a crooked sheriff who tried to pin a charge of murder on him.

Lance Clayton had found the Longrider Trail by reason of a faithless lady in financial straits. Lance had stuck up a saloon in her interest and, after turning the proceeds over to her, had left town two jumps ahead of a posse. Later, the lady vigorously repudiated him.

Of Doc Grimson's past nothing was known. That he had originally come from the East and was a man of culture and education, as well as an accomplished surgeon, seemed certain enough. But not even his partners had had a hint of the circumstances which had driven such a man West to live outside the law. They knew only that he combined complete fearlessness with one of the deadliest gun-hands since Wyatt Earp, and that he would stick with a partner up to hell's rearmost log and back again.

In the hands of such men a woman was more than safe. But that could not easily be explained to this girl who found herself friendless and alone in a wild country, and possession of whose person offered chances of ransom which would be welcomed by the El Lobo—and others.

While he reflected on these facts, the beat of horses' hoofs grew steadily louder and a moment later a group of riders leading saddled mounts stormed around the corner and flashed past without even a glance at the balcony. On their heels, however, hastened other men on foot. Lance saw the front door of the house across the way open, and heard a hiss from its dark shadow as the group on foot passed. They halted, gathering around the doorway. A murmur of low talk drifted up to Lance and he saw several of them turn their heads and look up toward the balcony.

After a moment the group moved over to a position just below him. "You take your ease, José," said one, "though the town is a-fire."

"A man is a man," Lance retorted angrily, "and not a slave!"

"Holá!" exclaimed the man, with a touch of mockery in his

19

tone, "Is this the voice of José who sits on his balcony with his young wife, Maria?"

Inside the window, the faintest rustle told Lance that the guns of Doc and Charlie were out. At the same moment, two realizations swept over him.

He realized that the man who spoke and the man who lived across the street, knew that he was not José. And he realized also that if the alarm was given now, they would have little chance. Their escape to the brush was cut off. The town was roused. And even if they attempted to fight their way through to the other side, the horses which had just swept by would run them down before they had covered half the distance.

HE GOT to his feet, José's knife flashing suddenly in his hand. "*Bueno!*" he said angrily. "I am not José. And does this concern thee, small dog whose tongue is long?"

"Ah-h!" The exclamation ran through the group on a sudden note of relief. A man laughed. The first speaker appeared somewhat taken aback, but recovered himself to say, "*Olá!* So it is not José who sits on José's balcony with José's wife! *Sinvergüenzas!* Oh ones without shame! Show us your face then, that we may know you!"

Lance said passionately, "Is it not permitted for one who comes from a distance to visit his—his sister, without having all the world poke its nose in at the window?"

"*Su hermana!*" the man repeated mocking. And another repeated, "*Su hermana—his sister!*" chuckling.

"*Bueno!*" Lance cried, furious. "It is enough. My patience is gone. You do not like 'sister,' eh? You like better another word?

Say that other word, amigo—that I may cut the heart from your dirty body. Afterwards, I will carve that word in the carcass of the old *borrachón* who led you here!"

Instinctively, the man below raised the rifle he held in his hand. "Big words are not big deeds," he retorted, but his voice sounded a little uncertain.

"Yah!" Lance spat at him. "You would like to shoot, eh? But it is not so that a man settles his quarrels. Listen, you others—now I will show you what a man of Hermosillo can do! Let him come up, that one—onto the balcony. I will put a scarf in his teeth, and in mine. Then, in this small space, we will fight, bound together by the scarf, until one is dead! Let him come now, quickly."

The man below was silent, so that another of the group said in a voice full of cruel amusement. *"Has entendido,* Juan?"

"This is not for another to fight for José's woman," the defensive reply sounded sullen. He added on a rising tone of triumph. "I will give your message to José, friend. His brother, who is one of El Lobo's men, is out there with the others and will come quickly."

The girl at Lance's side dropped her head into her hands. *"Madre de Dios!"* she moaned softly. "Have pity on me now!"

But Lance said, full of scorn, "Let him come—let them both come! I have a little brother," he flourished the knife in his hand, "who will speak to them softly and well!"

"We will see," the other shot him a venomous glance. "I go quickly."

Several of the group followed him, but a few lingered, thinking no doubt that this situation promised better drama than the hunt for the *Americanos.*

Lance leaned over the railing toward them. "Amigos," he said in a voice deadly soft. "We wish to be alone." Then added: "Unless—it is well understood—one of you wishes to fight the scarf duel, so that I may keep my hand in."

The group moved away at that, the most nimble of them being the old man. He got to his opened doorway quickly and as quickly closed it behind him.

Lance wiped the sweat from his brow. "Whew!" he breathed. Then he turned to the girl, taking on a mock-heroic air. "Let them come!" he declaimed. "The whole world is not too much to fight for such a one as you."

"I am shamed before my people," Doris replied brokenly. "I have only you to depend on now. You, and four others," she added, suppressing a giggle.

"Let us go to the ends of the world together then—" Lance wooed ardently—"a party of six." The giggle could no longer be suppressed at that.

Charlie Parr's voice came drily from the window. "If you Romeos are finished," it remarked. "We better go somewhere quick."

The girl murmured, suddenly sobered, "Go? Yes, but go—where?"

Lance shrugged a little wearily. *"Con Dios,"* he told her, repeating the Spanish phrase of farewell. "With God."

CHAPTER 3
FUGITIVE HOOFBEATS

T HEY WENT quietly down the stairs and out the back way, leaving the defamed and unfortunate José and Maria tied up in the front room. The back of the house gave onto an alley so narrow that it would have been impossible to walk two abreast. They turned to their left, for the street to the right had become a thoroughfare for traffic to and from the brush. Presently they came to a low adobe wall, which they climbed, dropping down into a paved back yard. This they traversed, moving silently as shadows, except for the click of one of the girl's heels, which caught on an inequality in the paving, making a sharp sound.

A woman's head appeared at the window. *"Quien es?"* she demanded in a quick frightened voice. "Who is it?"

Lance judged that she had not seen the others, who had gone on ahead.

"Quiet, Flower of the Night," he commanded in a whisper. "Do you not know that love walks and speaks on tiptoes?"

From the window, low feminine laughter greeted this impertinence, and he passed on. At the street they turned, keeping in the shadow of the walls. Voices brought them up sharply, crouching low behind a door stoop, as a party of searchers passed at the next corner. Then they went on, creeping through dark yards, following dingy alleys, darting from cover to cover. Danger lurked in every window, around every angle of the streets—for by now all Querida had been apprised of the search for them.

Scarcely anyone in that town who would not have turned them in, merely to do El Lobo a favor, but with the reward offered for them there would not be a man, woman or child who would not start a hue and cry at the merest suspected glimpse of them.

The thing in their favor was the fact that most of the town was already searching the brush for them, while those who remained behind had no doubt made their way to the central plaza, after the Latin fashion when there is excitement afoot.

The girl whispered in Lance's ear. "We're getting toward the center of town. Do they know that?"

"That's where we left the horses," Lance told her, "We haven't got a chance without them."

The girl stared at him wide-eyed, appeared about to speak, and then evidently changed her mind. It was plain that she was willing to accept their leadership unquestioningly, but she thought that going into the center of town was madness. They were sure to be seen, long before they could get within striking distance of the horses—if, indeed, the animals were still there!

A lone man came down the street, saw them, drew his breath in sharply and tried to duck into a darkened doorway. They found him plastered against the closed door, as though he were trying to merge his body with the wood. Lockjaw clipped him neatly over the head with a six-gun and they went on. But Lance saw that Doc Grimson had stopped and put something that glittered on the peon's chest. He judged it to be a twenty-dollar gold piece and thought he knew of one poor man who would wake up from an enforced sleep, rich beyond his dreams.

As they neared the plaza, three men came around a corner

and up the street toward them, walking arm in arm. They had evidently been drinking a little and they were singing. They did not recognize the figures before them until they were almost upon them.

"The man who runs or shouts will die," Doc Grimson said in a low voice. The three stood still, looking at the six-gun muzzles before them, fright bringing sobriety in its wake.

"Turn and walk before us," Doc directed briefly. "Remember that if one of you tries to run or make a suspicious sign, all of you will get bullets in your spines. March!"

The three turned and walked before them, keeping abreast. A moment later they met a man and a girl, who had eyes only for the three in front and so walked into the guns behind unsuspectingly.

"If you squeal just one little squeal," Doc told the girl, "Your man will die—and these three with him."

His words were just in time. She had drawn in her breath to let it out in a yell, but she let it hiss between her teeth instead.

They were nearly at the plaza now. The noise and light of it came at them around a jog in the narrow street. Doc Grimson pointed to the arched entrance of a courtyard, the great iron-studded doors of which were closed, making a short tunnel of darkness of the street. "We need some more, I think," he said, and motioned to the captives to get in out of sight.

They waited in the tunnel. Two more men came by and were taken in. Then a party of eight, four men and four women drifted down the street. One of the women started to scream, but Lockjaw Johnson clapped a ham-like hand over her mouth until the danger was passed. One of the men started to launch himself at Lockjaw but hauled up glaring impotently, as Flint's gun jammed into his stomach.

"Sorry to touch a woman," Doc Grimson said briefly, "but this was necessary, to save yourselves. Now listen to me well. We are going into the plaza to get horses—our horses." He scanned their faces closely as he said that, reading on those nearest the light the assurance that their mounts were still there. "You are coming with us—as a shield. The men will walk in a 'V' in front of us. The women will close us in behind us. No one will be watching the women. They may run or scream or make signals to the crowd. But this much I promise you, if that happens, ten men will lose their lives. There are five of us, each with two guns, and we do not miss. Remember that well. Now take your formation—two men strolling at the head of the 'V,' and walk across that plaza, laughing and talking, so that no man will notice anything unusual. It is your only chance to live."

SO IT was done. Their bodyguard looked a little pale-faced and strained, but nobody tried anything—nobody risked the menace of the guns in the center. A few of the crowd in the plaza looked at them curiously, and Lance saw one man stare, grow pale and turn excitedly to say something to the people near them. But they were well past him when that happened—almost up to the half-a-dozen men who lounged near their horses.

They were entirely careless, those guards. It was plain that they didn't believe for a moment they would be needed. Not even the five mad gringos would risk walking back into the hornet's nest which Querida had become.

"Not too close, amigos," one of them warned as the wedge of the "V" approached. "You might—" He broke off, staring, as his eye fell on the men in the center.

"Get your hands up quickly," Doc Grimson snapped.

The other guards whirled, faces unbelieving. One of them raised his rifle to fire. Charlie Parr's right-hand gun spoke between the heads of the two shields in front of him and the guard yowled as the bullet smashed the bone of his upper arm. The two men standing in front of Charlie swayed sidewise, deafened by the explosion near their ears, and then broke in panic.

From then on the plaza was a scene of the wildest possible confusion. Women screamed. Panic-stricken men stumbled over one another getting to cover. Others, braver, reached for guns which the crowd prevented them from using effectively. But at the core of this confusion there was activity of the most exquisite orderliness. The five remaining guards were disarmed with astonishing simultaneousness. And within five seconds of the first shot, the five men were in the saddle, one of them holding the reins of a sixth horse belonging to one of the guards.

Those who were not too frightened to see anything, then saw a big blond young man with wide, powerful shoulders reach down and sweep a breathless girl to the pommel before him. A salvo of shots whistled over the heads of the crowd, and an instant later the gringos were clattering at full gallop down the nearest side street. It was observed only that two of the men rode behind the man with the girl and two at his side, shielding her from fire. Then the whole group raced around a turn in the street and were lost to sight.

CHAPTER 4
PARDNERS FIVE

G RAY LIGHT materialized like a ghost from the heart of the darkness. The face of the girl beside Lance showed oval, magnolia-pale. Doc Grimson's sombrero was a patch intensely black against the lightened ground. One of Flint's boots, protruding from behind a nearby rock, took form. Charlie Parr's soft snore was no more than an overtone to the silence.

In the east a shaft of color shot upward, spread, expanded into crimson rays. Doc Grimson came awake like a cat, luminous gray eyes wide and instantly comprehending, body turning in a light, lithe movement that brought him facing toward the ridge. He slid softly forward, beside Lance, to where he could see over the top.

A cloud of white dust on the road a mile away became a dozen riders, pushing leg-weary horses. That would be the men who had pounded past the night before on the trail which led to the mountains and the Bar Bullion Mine. They were return-ing now on horses ridden nearly to death, but Doc and Lance guessed that one of them at least had ridden on, picking up relay mounts at scattered *haciendas* in the hills. What El Lobo commandered, men gave willingly.

To the right, miles away, Querida's adobes showed—a huddle

of gray in the clear morning light. Beyond them, faint, on the stage road leading north to the Border, another dust-cloud showed.

Something glinted from a house-top in Querida—flashed short, then long, then short again. Mirror signals to the mountains. Presently, on a distant ridge a thin column of smoke rose, disappeared, rose again. The hills were talking back to the town.

Lance said soberly. "You had it figured out about right, Doc. I bet there won't be a place for a hundred miles around where they ain't lookin' out for five gringos and a girl.

Doc looked rueful. "I don't know that figuring it out did much good," he answered. "We still don't know where to go. The way it is, we can't get either to the Border or to the mine."

The others had come awake and now were crawling up to join the two on the ridge. Doris Enderby, who was not accustomed to wake at the crack of day, slept on, exhausted by the events of the night before.

"If it wasn't for the girl," Charlie Parr said thoughtfully, "I'd say to ride for the Border. Likely we could fight our way through. Maybe that's the only thing to do, anyway."

"Not a chance," Flint disagreed. "We could do it—we could take either trail, riding like hell and changing horses wherever we found some. With these signals going out, El Lobo would be on our trail within an hour, but he couldn't catch us. And a few peons pot-shooting at us as we fanned past wouldn't do any harm. But with the girl it's different. She couldn't stand the pace. It'd be suicide to try it."

"All right, then," Charlie Parr returned drily. "Let's just stay here, where we're safe."

Flint made no answer to that—there being none to make—and the five started at one another with eyes which all contained the same wordless thought. They were trapped. El Lobo had no need to stir out of his den in order to look for them. He need only wait, patiently, with the help of his wine and his women, until word came in that they had been seen. Then he would take the trail, and the end was sure.

"Maybe we could lay up here until dark and then take the trail, travelin' only at night," Lance offered dubiously.

"They'll be out cutting for sign within an hour," said Charlie Parr. "And we left plenty of it along our trail."

"Anyway," Flint said, "we'd have to stick to the trails at night—we wouldn't get far without being noticed."

Doc said slowly, "There'd be one way."

They looked at him inquiringly. He motioned over his shoulder. "The desert," he said simply.

"Say! That's right," Lance exclaimed. "It's a shorter way; it leads close to the mine, and it's the last trail they'd think we'd take!"

CHARLIE PARR looked at his hands, as though he found something particularly interesting there. "Sure," he said finally. "And there wouldn't be anybody out there to send signals back about us."

Flint Maddox looked over his shoulder in the direction of that pitiless inferno of sand as though he were seeking to divine what lay within its barren, waterless expanse. "What about sign?" he asked at length. "If they cut for it now, they'll find our trail clear enough out there."

"Leave that to Charlie," Lockjaw broke his silence to say proudly. "He'll fool 'em."

Charlie looked at him a little wearily, but replied to the question in the others' glances with a noncommittal, "Might be done."

"I've got it," Doc said with sudden enthusiasm. "It's simple. We split. That'll fool El Lobo. Four of you take the mountain trail to the mine. You'll get through. Anyway, some of you will. I'll hit the desert with Miss Enderby. Nobody'll be behind us and nobody'll be in the way. That way, the girl'll be safe and you'll be free to ride."

Charlie Parr looked at him as one looks at someone who has made a poor joke. "*You'll* hit the desert with Miss Enderby, will you?" he inquired sardonically.

"Look here, boys," Doc said with an apologetic air. "I hate like thunder to be grabbing off the easy job for myself—and sending you off where you'll have hell a-popping all the way, but I'm afraid that's the way it sizes up. This desert thing is safe enough, but it's going to be a hard trip on that girl. If she gets too much sun, or gets exhausted on the way, I think I ought to be along to take care of her. We kind of owe it to her, now, to get her through in the best shape possible."

Lance sought Charlie Parr's gaze and held it a brief instant, the beginning of a smile flickering about the corners of his mouth. When he looked away, he found Flint staring at him, comprehension in the depths of his melancholy brown eyes.

Lance permitted his smile to become an ironic grin. So Doc was picking the safe job for himself, was he? Just like Doc, that was! Oh, sure!

Doc must be getting childish. Did he really think he could put that over on them? Did he think he was the only one who knew anything about deserts—the only one who knew what it was to face the remorseless blaze of the sun in a land without water, his tongue thicker than a hundred furry caterpillars, and fire in his tortured veins instead of blood?

Only so much water a horse could pack, with a rider, too. And a slender bit of a girl who would need the lion's share of that water! She'd get through, yes. Someway, Doc would see to that. And Doc? Well, if he didn't happen to make it…. Oh, no, it wasn't good enough—not by a good many burning miles, it wasn't!

Lance reached over and patted Doc's shoulder comfortingly. "You'll get over it, Doc," he said. "Just take it easy. This high, dry climate is hard on a lot of people."

Charlie Parr said, "Likely it's that there *tequila* he was drinkin' last night."

"The trouble with these smart rannies," Flint Maddox remarked placidly, "is that they get to under-rating ordinary folks' brains."

Lockjaw started, uncomprehending. He was not a desert man. Doc Grimson was wearing his poker face, and said nothing. He did not have to have it explained to him further that he had lost *that* jackpot. He had sought to fool them into letting him take the major risk. But they were on to him now—and he knew that whatever danger one of them would face, the others would face also!

DORIS ENDERBY stirred and sat up, staring around her in bewilderment. Even after a disheveled night in the open, she looked disturbingly pretty. Lance slipped down to her. "Cold chuck this mornin', lady," he told her cheerfully. "How do you feel—ready to do a little light traveling?"

Fifteen minutes later they were on their way, following down the shelter of a draw. Behind them, from the town, groups of riders had come out, separating and circling with their eyes on the ground.

The draw led them near to a small adobe shack, to which their attention was attracted by a violent odor of pig-sty and the unmistakable fragrance of goat. Lance looked at Charlie, who nodded, saying: "Might as well. They'll follow our sign this far, anyway."

With Lockjaw, Lance climbed to the edge of the ravine. A man, lean, unshaven and ragged lounged before the doorway of the one-room adobe. A boy had begun to herd half a dozen goats out toward their daily pasture. A slatternly woman came to the door and threw a pan of dirty water onto the ground outside. No one else was in sight.

Lockjaw pointed to where several scrawny chickens pecked forlornly at the ground about the shack. *"Pollos!"* he announced with satisfaction.

Lance said, "Let's go." They pulled themselves up over the edge and began to walk toward the shack. The man got to his feet suddenly and stood staring at them with an expression of fright. The boy looked as though he wanted to run but didn't dare. Lance motioned him to come over and after a moment he did so, trembling.

"We won't hurt you, my son," Lance told him, "but we have to tie you up for a while."

Neither the man nor the woman made any resistance. Lying bound, with the boy, on the bed, they looked scared, out of their wits until they saw the amount of silver which Lance tossed down beside them. Then their bewilderment took on a different cast.

He found half of a moldy ham on a shelf and some beans and coffee. He took these and a couple of half-filled wineskins. When he got outside he found that the vigorous squawking he had heard had not been misleading. Lockjaw had a chicken in each hand.

They went down to the others then and Lockjaw proudly held out his capture. "Look! *Pollos!*" he said, "and *vino!*" He tied the chickens behind his saddle and went over to Lance, taking one of the wine-skins from him. "Ever see how they drink out of these?" he asked Charlie Parr, and put the skin to his mouth.

Charlie slapped it from his hand. "Jawhead!" he exclaimed angrily. "What are you tryin' to do, kill yourself? Don't you know where we're ridin' to?"

Lockjaw looked abashed but evidently didn't in the least know what Charlie meant. He looked at the wine which was pouring from the skin. "You've spilt it all now, Charlie," he pointed out regretfully.

"Pick up the skin and pour the rest of the wine out of it,"

Charlie directed curtly, "an' don't start drinkin' wine on no desert trips."

Lockjaw stared and opened his mouth to speak, but closed it again. This was the first intimation he had had that the rest of them, as well as Doc, were taking the desert trail.

But Charlie Parr was paying no attention to him. He was staring at the spreading stain of the wine on the hard earth and there was a frown on his face. After a moment, however, he shrugged his shoulders and the party moved off. If he had followed his impulse to cover that stain over, it might have been better for them.

But at the moment not even Charlie was sure why he regretted that the wine had been spilt, and a few seconds later the incident had gone from his mind, crowded out by the necessity for covering their trail.

So far the course of the ravine had led them in the direction of the mountains. Now Charlie led the way out across some rocks and followed a winding course around a flinty hillside for several hundred yards. From then on their course was a maze of back-trailing, turns onto rock, sudden slides into sandy arroyos, and painful progress through chapparal. The country was bare and cover scarce, but the seasoned old-timer who led them took advantage of every favorable conformation of ground and it seemed certain that they had not been seen.

Eventually, the twisting trail led out to a creek, where they replenished their canteens and washed and filled the wine-skins. Two hours later their horses stood on low rimrock which edged a gray-white, contorted plain out of which rose a blast of suffocating heat, like a furnace breath. The desert was before them.

CHAPTER 5
EL LOBO AGAIN

HEAT BLASTED down on them from above, ringed them round like a hidden fire, beat up at them from the parched and burning ground. It sucked up the sweat from their faces, leaving dry, stinging salt in its place. It danced its devil's shimmy over every rock, on the blazing beds of the salt hollows, above the wavering outlines of tortured mesquite and the sprawling cruel forms of the cactus.

Light poured over them blindingly from the metal cup of the sky. It lanced at them from every glint of mica, from the burning metal of their equipment and the very sheen of their horses' hides. It lashed at them from every sand-polished surface; launched itself in an unendurable glare from the incandescent stretches of the soda flats; tore with subtle fingers at shrinking skins; drove tortured eyes deep into red-rimmed sockets. There was no escape from it, never an instant of relief.

Dust rose in clouds about them, seeped into clothing, gritted on the skin beneath. Dust covered their faces, whitened eyebrows and lashes, coated nostrils and throats with its maddening film. Dust—as never-ending, as relentless and unremitting, as the furnace breath of the heat, the intolerable blaze of the light.

For the hundredth time, Lance glanced anxiously at Doris Enderby. Like the rest of them, she rode now in silence, chin, mouth and nose muffled in a bandanna for protection against the dust and the scorching dryness of the air. But the skin between the neckerchief top and the brim of the fancy Stetson which topped the riding outfit she had donned to meet Bart McAllister showed fiery under the film of dust and her eyes were deep-sunken and strained. From time to time her shoulders slumped wearily or her back twisted in involuntary protest at the agony of muscles unaccustomed to such long hours in the saddle.

Game, Lance decided, again. The girl was game clear through. And that was the danger. She'd keep her saddle like a thoroughbred until the last vestige of strength, of vitality, of nerve was gone out of her. Then she'd fold up for good.

Game, all right. She had taken last night's business like a good soldier. And she had begun this desert trip with a sort of debonair eagerness that had puzzled Lance. He supposed that, although she had spent her childhood on the Border, she didn't understand what the desert could be. Yet there was more than that to it, somehow. There had been a sort of light in her eyes—he fumbled at explaining its quality even to himself. She had looked almost like a girl going to her wedding!

Lance looked up toward Charlie Parr, riding in the lead, and wished that he would call a halt. They had rested briefly for lunch. He was afraid that Charlie would not realize how tired this girl already was. But even as he looked Charlie rode down into an ancient dry wash where an overhanging rock and some stunted mesquite gave a derisory appearance of shade, and pulled up. Four o'clock. The sand, the rocks burned up through

All at once the others also saw the thing that held Charlie's gaze—the mounting cloud of dust. El Lobo!

their bootsoles; sitting on them was like sitting on a heated frying pan.

Lance got a slicker and a coat from his saddlebags and spread them for the girl. He saw that she was afraid to lie down for fear they would guess how tired she was, so he made her stretch out.

"Water stop," Charlie announced cheerfully, nodding significantly at Lance. He raised his canteen to the girl and said, "Here's luck, lady."

He drank impolitely by way of example, tilting the canteen high, with his old Adam's apple working in leisurely swallows. But Lance saw that the lips under the flowing white mustache were pressed tightly together and knew that not a drop of that precious fluid was escaping from the mouth of the bottle.

He handed his own canteen to the girl. She took it, took a small swallow, and handed it back to him.

"That'll never do," he told her. "You need more than that." He forced her to drink again.

"I'll say you need more than that," Lockjaw exclaimed, swabbing his forehead with a bandanna. "I thought I'd saw some hot weather, but dang me if I ever see anything that was a patch on this." He up-ended his canteen and let the water gurgle down his throat.

Charlie Parr's hand jerked in a sudden, involuntary movement and the glare of sheer outraged feelings leaped into his eyes. But when the girl, attracted by his movement, looked at him, he was merely staring out across the desert. His face was impassive.

Lance said quickly, "Now you lie down and close your eyes a minute." He pushed her gently backward and put her sombrero over her eyes.

Lockjaw was tilting the bottle for another swig, when he found Charlie's gaze upon him—a gaze unhampered now by the possibility that Doris might read its meaning. It arrested Lockjaw's hand in mid-air as though it had been turned to stone. He stared in utter bewilderment.

LANCE CAUGHT his attention. In silent pantomime he

pressed his lips tightly together and went through the pretense of drinking, working his throat violently. Lockjaw stared. Lance pointed to the girl and nodded his head affirmatively, then pointed to himself and the others and shook his head. Comprehension dawned on Lockjaw's long, horse-like face, and a slow tide of red stained his wooden features. He started to speak, caught the warning shake of Charlie Parr's head and closed his lips.

From then on he sat in the greatest dejection. When they got going again he rode up alongside Charlie Parr. "Sorry about that water, Charlie," he muttered, looking shame-faced. "I didn't—"

"Not your fault," Charlie cut him off gruffly. "I forgot you wasn't used to deserts."

"I thought everybody was drinkin' an'—"

"Dry up! No harm's done. Just take it kind of easy—drink in sips, you know. We're all goin' to need all the water we can get before this is over. Which if there's a water hole on this desert I don't know where it is."

Sunset came after an endless time. The heat ceased to beat down from above, and, though the blast from below seemed worse than ever, existence became more tolerable because of the disappearance of the all-encircling hideous brightness.

When darkness came they made camp and had some cold food. Lance could see that Doris Enderby was suffering an agony of tortured muscles and intense fatigue, but she made no complaint and even made an attempt during the meal to recapture her normally high-spirited and valorous air. The food and a generous portion of water revived her somewhat. At the end of it, she began to talk optimistically of the pleasures of arriving at the mine after such a difficult trip.

"We'll be quite safe there," she ended. "I know Bart—Mr. McAllister—has trained a force of Mexicans and Yaquis who can easily guard the mine, and at least there'll be plenty of food and water. I feel already that I could drink gallons and gallons of water, don't you? Believe me," she went on earnestly, "I know that nothing can repay such friendship as you've shown me, but—well, if there's anything I have that you can use, it's yours. Anything! In fact, I don't think I shall ever be quite happy again until I find a way to—I won't say 'pay you back' because that couldn't ever be done—but show you how much I appreciate.... Oh, it's impossible to say it, but you know what I mean. Anyway," she added, smiling, "it's going to be fun to have you at the Bar Bullion. Bart's going to help me turn the place upside down for you when he hears what you've done."

"You think a good deal of—I mean to say you've got a lot of confidence in that superintendent of yours?" Charlie Parr threw out the question with a casual air.

"Indeed I have!" the girl responded with a flash of animation. "He's one of the best, and a fine man. Father trusted him absolutely, and so do I."

Charlie Parr nodded without replying and for a moment there was silence—a silence during which the men occupied themselves variously and avoided each others' eyes. All except Lockjaw. He stared with unblinking gaze at Doris Enderby a moment, then asked bluntly: "How come he didn't meet you down at Querida then?"

The girl flushed a little and then said, frowning, "I wish I knew. It worries me a little. I—I hope nothing serious has happened to him."

Nobody said anything to that, and in order to break the constraint, Lance stretched and said, "I reckon we better get some rest. I bet that there old mule-skinner"—he indicated Charlie—"ain't goin' to give us much of it."

Charlie nodded grimly. "We'll ride at midnight," he said in confirmation.

Lance looked a little surprised. He had expected, after the day they had had, that Charlie would give the girl until two or three o'clock in the morning to sleep. Evidently the old-timer was concerned about something. Did he think that El Lobo might strike their trail? There had been no signs of him all day.

But when he stretched out on the hot ground, staring up at the blazing desert stars, it was not of El Lobo that he thought but of the mine superintendent, Bart McAllister, and the expression in Doris Enderby's eyes when she spoke of him. It puzzled Lance. She couldn't very well be in love with the man, for she herself had said that she had not seen him since she was a child. Still, girl's were funny. Perhaps....

He had heard something about Bart McAllister, as had the others. He had the reputation of being a tough customer—a ruthless driver of the Yaquis who worked for him, and a hard man in his dealings with the outside world. It was a little queer, given that sort of man, that the mine should be so unprofitable, and that El Lobo had been allowed to rob it with impunity. Still, it might not be McAllister's fault. No use judging the man before the evidence was in. He hoped the girl was not going to be too disappointed in McAllister... or did he? Well, anyway—part of him hoped that. The other part could not help wishing.... He put the thought aside.

One thing was certain, anyway, he thought as his eyes closed—Doc Grimson and Charlie Parr did not share the girl's confidence in her superintendent. What had happened to the man, anyway? Had he sloped off with what remained of the mine's profits when he heard that the girl was coming to investigate him? If so, they might find the guards disbanded and themselves again at the mercy of El Lobo and his men.

And then, it seemed almost before that last thought had completed itself in his mind, he felt Charlie's gnarled hand on his shoulder. It was midnight.

LANCE HAD to help Doris Enderby into the saddle. She was much too stiff to climb up by herself. Even with his help the uncontrollable grimace on her face told him the pain of her muscles was nearly unbearable.

The going was harder and slower, but it seemed like easy travel after the inferno of the day. They would ride, Lance told the girl, until the sun was well up, then find a place that offered some sort of shade to lay up until late afternoon. She'd get a real rest then, and afterwards traveling at night, and before the sun got high in the morning, the journey would not be so punishing. He wanted her to have that thought to hold to—to help her through the long hours ahead.

He wondered how much she was beginning to feel thirst, but that was a subject of which, by tacit consent, nobody spoke. Lance himself had begun to feel the cry in him for water—the thirst which is not thirst but an inner need, a calling out of moisture-starved tissues. He knew from experience the agony that could become and his heart shrank from the possibility that this girl should come to know it also. Twice during the night, he forced her to take a sip from his canteen, pretending to do the same thing himself. In the darkness, it was easy to slip the stopper in, so as not to waste even a few drops against his closed lips.

Nonetheless, the night was endless and long before dawn Lance was riding at the girl's side to hold her in the saddle during those moments when sleep overcame her irresistibly, despite the world of pain in which she lived. Lance's own muscles grew cramped, leaning out to hold her up. Then suddenly the air was gray and the dawn came up, blaring into full day almost before the first trumpet notes of color had formed themselves above the distant eastern hills. Dawn, and the promise, not too far distant, of rest.

Charlie Parr turned in his saddle, pulled up, stared at the trail behind them. And then, all at once, the others also saw the thing which held his gaze. Far off, faint even in this clear dry land of vast distances, but unmistakable, was a mounting cloud of dust!

El Lobo!

THEY STARED at each other out of eyes gone strained and desperate. El Lobo and his gang would come on fast, fresh mounts, no doubt, with extra horses to change to when the first had been ridden to death. El Lobo would carry water—plenty of water. And there was no place to fight, no chance to make a successful stand. If they were caught, they would be caught out in this vast, flat, cruel expanse—exhausted, fevered and feeble with thirst and heat; so agonized that in the end El Lobo's bullets must come as a final mercy.

Lance read that in the others' eyes, knew it out of the depths of his own young experience. He felt the bitter, wracking thirst clamor up in him. It seemed strange to him and somehow unjust that this should be the end of so many happy adventures—that the five should go out through such a senseless hell of heat, of torture, of madness. Oddly, in that moment, the girl for which they had been willing to risk everything, ceased to count with him. Only the faces of the other four were in his mind's eye now....

For one moment of weakness, he wanted to stop where they were and wait it out. That way at least they would meet El Lobo's bullets sane and whole, like men. But the impulse passed. Whatever hell's ordeal might be in store for them, they'd have to play their string out like men. Play it out together, inseperably as they had lived.

Charlie Parr said: "We'll stop here for a mite of breakfast." His face had grown impassive again.

"Breakfast!" Doc Grimson exclaimed cheerfully. "That'll do pretty good with me!" That was a good, optimistic lie.

Nobody, Lance knew, wanted food. But a ration of food

meant a ration of water, and that was good. Food could be choked down, just to have the water.

Doris Enderby looked at the distant dust-cloud with a hint of terror in her eyes. "Is it—are they—far?" she asked.

Lance knew that her impulse was to press on at once, in a hurry. The idea of stopping for breakfast with El Lobo on their trail was something scarcely to be thought of.

"They're a hard day's ride back of us," he told her. "Don't you get worried. We'll have to keep moving right along, but they won't catch us. You mustn't try to hurry the desert, you know. It doesn't like it. It gets riled up, when you try to hurry it, and does bad things to you. Easy's the word. There's nothing to worry about."

The horses had their nostrils and throats swabbed out with a damp rag and Charlie rationed them oats and water. They were already a gaunted, leg-weary lot, but Lance saw that they were holding up pretty well. Even the mount they had taken for Doris had turned out to be a good one—a tough, wiry little animal, well fitted for this hard, dry country. They'd have use for every bit of stamina in them before this thing was over.

It was when they came to take their own rations of water that Lance first saw that Lockjaw wasn't drinking. He was putting the canteen to his closed lips as Charlie Parr had first done.

Lance got him aside. "How long since you've had a drink?" he asked.

Lockjaw looked stubborn, "I just had one," he asserted.

"Is that the kind of drink you've been having since yesterday afternoon?"

"Hell," Lockjaw boasted, "you don't have to worry about me, Lance. It don't take much water to keep me goin'. I'm used to it."

"You take a drink and you take it now, or I'll bust your fool jaw for you."

Lockjaw grinned through cracked lips. "Aw, now, Lance," he protested, "What's the use? I been cracked on the jaw by experts. It don't have no effect on me whatever."

Lance called Charlie Parr and Doc Grimson. "You danged jawhead!" Charlie Parr exploded. "What you tryin' to do—kill yourself? Hell! We've all drunk twice as much water as that drink you had yesterday. If that's what you're tryin' to make up for, you've already done it. You go ahead and drink."

"I just had a drink," Lockjaw lied stolidly. And no amount of persuasion could cajole him from that position or force him to swallow any water.

In the end, Charlie Parr threw his hands over his head and said: "Die of thirst, then—you idjit!" But Lance could see that he was as worried as the rest of them. When Lockjaw got an idea in his head, dynamite couldn't jar it loose. He had drunk too much water and shamed himself. Hence he would drink no more water at all. There was no sense in it—but that was Lockjaw.

After an hour's rest they moved on. The sun was already high, and the hammer strokes of its heat increased in force and intensity every moment. The trial by fire and light and dust had begun again.

CHAPTER 6
DESERT HELL

THROUGHOUT THE day they slogged ahead. Where the going was soft they dismounted and went on foot, to take the killing load from their weary horses. Charlie Parr sat down and hacked the high heels from his boots, and the rest followed his example.

By noon, Doris Enderby was plainly reaching the limit of her resistance. Lance saw her falter and stagger, walking beside her horse; saw her sway dangerously in the saddle.

Charlie Parr called a halt. With Lance's help he rigged a stretcher made of rope and a couple of ponchos, and slung it between two horses. They made Doris Enderby lie on it and made a shade for her head. She protested feebly, but she was too far gone to make much resistance.

Doggedly, hour by hour they scuffed on, while thirst—the immense, all-embracing thirst of the desert—grew in them like an inner fire. Lance knew that the water was getting dangerously low. They had used the greater amount of it for the horses, as desert-wise men will, and there could not be much left. He left the rationing of the water to Charlie Parr, trying to put the thought of it out of his head, concentrating on the sheer painful task of putting one foot after another, or of sitting steady and easy in the saddle during the periods when they rode. Hour by hour, with set jaws, they plodded on, while behind them the dust-cloud grew, crept closer.

The hot sand burned up through Lance's boot soles, bit at his feet where the leather had chafed the flesh raw. He could feel the blood trickle and his feet grow wet with it. It was like walking in liquid fire.

The white glare tore at his eyeballs. Dust coated the parchment dryness of his throat and nose, crept toward the membrane of his lungs. It was painful to breathe.

Sunset came. Charlie measured out water—a generous portion for Doris, a derisory two swallows for the men, and half of that for himself. Lockjaw declined his portion, alleging that he had just drunk from his canteen. Lockjaw's eyes were fiery red, his eyelids swollen, and his lips cracked and bleeding. His throat was evidently in such bad shape that he could scarcely speak his refusal.

Charlie Parr cursed and stormed at him. Lockjaw set his teeth and preserved silence.

Lance said: "What about you, Charlie? I saw you cut your ration in half."

"I know how much water I need," Charlie told him gruffly. "I was crossin' deserts when you was still wet behind the ears."

The dust-cloud behind them had grown bigger. The distant sanctuary of the mountains seemed almost as distant as ever. At this rate, El Lobo would come up with them before dawn. He must be setting a killing pace.

The nightmare of the darkness began. The hot, breathless, dusty desert dark, through which exhausted animals and tortured men stumbled, staggered, fought their way forward. And thirst was a growing madness.

Lance's veins were burning channels through which fire ran. Every nerve and tissue in his body clamored, yelled, shouted, for water. He felt his throat closing and his tongue beginning to swell. There were still a few drops of water in his canteen—suppose he took them now? They were his, weren't they? He could go without water later. Besides, El Lobo would be in range by sunrise. What was the use of going through the agony? They wouldn't have much use for water tomorrow!

He set his teeth and shook his head. That wasn't the thing to think about. He must think of keeping going. Chin down, to help his breathing—first one foot, then the other. Count. I'll do just fifty more steps. Fifty. Now another fifty. It isn't much water—might as well have it now. Not water, but life. Precious drops like warm, dull diamonds. Nobody would know, in the darkness, if he drank them. Wet, over his dry tongue—cooling his fiery veins. No! Do you hear? No! Fifty. Do a hundred this time….

The girl, stirred on her stretcher, moaned. She was in the semi-torpor of exhaustion. Thirst must be tearing at her, too. What was the use? She couldn't last, and neither could they.

Lockjaw began to sing. His hoarse, cracked voice came grotesquely out of the darkness ahead—a tuneless croaking.

After a little Lance stumbled on him. He was down on his knees, digging in the sand. "Water!" he croaked. "It's right under the surface. I can hear it running. Help me dig, Lance."

They threw him down then, forced a wet rag between his

black, swollen lips. The horses, halted, dropped in their tracks. When they had tended to Lockjaw, the men did likewise.

Lockjaw was better after half an hour's rest and more water. Charlie measured out water for everybody. They swabbed out the nostrils and throats of the animals. Then, wearily, doggedly, they got into motion again.

SUNRISE—LIKE A brazen blare in the east. They looked back. The dust-cloud which was El Lobo, and death, was a full three hours behind them. It looked close, though—so close in that clear air, that Doris Enderby gasped.

"Thought so," said Charlie Parr through dry lips. "Danged near killed themselves and had to ease down."

Lance looked at the mountains. They looked close now, too—but he knew they were nearly a day's march away. Looking at them, foreseeing the endless desert miles in between, his heart failed him. They had a chance—just a chance—to make it now, if they could hold out. A chance—but at what a price! At the cost of their heart's blood; at the cost of the last drained drop of vitality in them; at the cost of becoming staggering shells of men—tortured, maddened, spent!

It would have been better if El Lobo had come faster—better to pay their final debt, here, in the dawn. Nothing, not even life itself, was worth this effort. So Lance thought, and clamped his teeth shut to keep the thought within himself.

Charlie Parr made them rest a short half hour; made them go through the pretense of eating; measured out the last of the water.

When they got ready to start again the horse which had

carried Doris refused to get up. They left him, hoping that El Lobo would mercifully have enough water, or that after a rest, the wiry little animal might find strength enough to make his way to the mountains.

It was an omen of what might come. Their own horses, selected as they had been for speed and stamina, grain-fed and coddled against just such emergencies as this, were in a sorry state. They might not last the day.

They went on. Lance wondered if he looked as badly off as the rest. Flint Maddox's face was a drawn mask, with the lips puffing out and the eyes deep-sunk. Charlie Parr looked like death. You could see that the years had left their mark on him—that in him exhaustion went bone-deep, without the recuperative powers of youth to ward it off. For Charlie that half hour's rest might just as well not have been.

Lockjaw looked even worse. Only his iron strength could have brought him so far through the waterless ordeal he had imposed on himself. They made him take his share of water now, but a good deal of the damage had been done.

Of them all, except the girl, Doc Grimson looked least ravaged. That man's muscles were supple steel and the effortless grace of all his movements conserved his vitality enormously.

Looking at him, Lance felt ashamed of his own weakness and took new heart for the soul-trying work ahead.

They went on. The sun crept up in the sky; light blazed from a thousand brilliant surfaces. Dust clung about them in a suffocating cloud hour after hour. And always behind them the gray column that marked El Lobo's progress. Was it gaining?

Were they holding their own? Lance ceased to care. His feet were molten lumps of lead. His skin was a prickly garment of torture. His sombrero clamped around his head like an iron band. Savagely, he fought the impulse to toss it aside, free himself of that intolerable burden.

Then the water dreams began. Lakes showed their blue and siren surfaces in the distance. Sparkling rivers ran into the desert. Hidden water courses ran under his feet, the sound of their rushing a sweet madness in his ears. With some remnant of sanity, he remembered Lockjaw's state of the night before and fought the almost irresistible temptation to kneel and dig with his hands.

Water! The thought, the vision, the feel and taste of it obsessed him. Twenty times he would have wandered off after some mirage, except that he knew he had to follow Charlie Parr. He thought about that in the early stages of the madness, fixed it in his mind. He must follow Charlie Parr. Whatever happened he must keep in the column. Follow Charlie. Water. Fifty more steps. Ah, but the water around him! Just off at the left, there. The most beautiful, tempting sight he had ever imagined. He had to go to it, bathe in it, sink his fevered temples in it, feel its cool delicious flow on his cracked lips and swollen tongue.

Insanely, he broke into a trot. He had to get up to Charlie and tell him about that water. Charlie hadn't seen it, evidently. He saw Doc Grimson looking back at him, with a curious expression in his eyes. It sobered him, somehow. His mind cleared of the water images long enough to let him set his teeth and drop back to his place beside the girl.

That girl was always wanting him to ride. She kept trying to get down from the litter. What was the matter with her? Wasn't she comfortable? What good would it do him to ride? Water was what he needed.

He stumbled and fell. Water ran before him on the desert, just out of his mouth's reach. If only he could inch himself up to it....

HE FELT a canteen at his mouth. A few drops of water, warm, brackish but like a dream of paradise, trickled over his lips onto his swollen tongue. A voice said in a low tone—was it Doc's? "Afraid of this. He kept giving most of his share to the girl."

But where was the water coming from? There wasn't any more. He shut his mouth tight. Somebody was trying to give him more than his share of water. That wouldn't do. Follow Charlie.

He struggled to his knees. Doc Grimsons' face came to him through a red haze. "No!" he whispered to it. "No—no water."

Somebody took him by the shoulders and flung him onto his back. His eyes closed involuntarily against the dreadful brightness of the sky. Water trickled into his mouth—delicious, life-giving drops on his tongue, back in raw dryness of his aching throat.

He lay still for a while, then had the strength to ask: "Where—water come—from?"

"Lockjaw had a little," Doc's voice told him, "and I kept a little in my canteen because I had more than I needed. Here, take a little more."

He could swallow now. Strength began to come back into him. He got up and wanted to go on. Doc made him rest a little more and tried to get him to take some more water, but he refused that, although the cry of his body for it was almost not to be borne. He could see that Lockjaw and Flint and Charlie needed water as badly as he did. They tried to refuse it, but Doc made them drink, after he had scanned Lance's face and estimated the strength that was coming back into him.

Doris Enderby declined indignantly to take another drop. She said she was stronger than any of them. She insisted on walking, so they could ride. But a look at the staggering horses was enough to put that idea out of their heads. Those horses couldn't carry anybody.

They went on. Lance still walked through a red haze, but he could see Charlie Parr's back and he kept after it, putting one foot before the other, using all his will-power to achieve every step.

Then he saw Charlie Parr go down. He made his feet go faster then, somehow, running up to help Charlie. It was a long way, but he made it. He put his arm under Charlie's body and tried to lift him, but found him too heavy. Charlie got to his knees, with an agonized effort and Lance dropped his gaze rather than look at the shame in Charlie Parr's eyes.

Lockjaw and Doc came up then and they managed to get Charlie tied into the saddle of Lance's stallion, because he looked stronger than the other horses.

Flint Maddox began to wander off to the side—off into the desert. Doc and Lance got him back, with an effort that almost did for both of them. He insisted in hoarse, urgent whispers that there was water out there, but let himself be led back into line.

Then they were going on again. Doris Enderby walked beside Flint, holding onto his sleeve when he tried to veer off again. Lance followed Doc Grimson's back now. It was hard to keep him in sight because Lockjaw kept weaving across the hole in the red haze and shutting off the sight of Doc's back. Lance realized vaguely that Lockjaw must be staggering. He hoped he wouldn't fall—he'd be heavier to pick up than Charlie Parr.

Lance kept on, ducking his head from side to side to keep Doc's back in sight. Then, all of a sudden, he lost it and couldn't find it again. He guessed Doc must have gotten ahead and tried to hurry. Lockjaw disappeared next. That was bad. Then he found a red wall in front of him and realized that the ground sloped up. He stagged on several steps before he realized what that meant. They were out of the desert! Before long, somewhere, there must be water! He tried to cheer, but no sound came out of his throat.

Then, at last, there was water—a clear stream of it, rippling down in cascades, shining and dancing in the sunlight. Lance shut his eyes, to keep the vision out. He didn't want to be fooled again. But when he opened them again he realized that this water had a subtly different quality from the visions that had tortured him before. It was real, solid. The sound of it was different. Then he saw that Doc Grimson had stopped beside it and was motioning for the rest of them to come on. Not drinking—but waiting for them!

"Take it easy," Doc croaked at them, when they had come up. "A little at a time."

They sat down beside that sparkling stream and cupped the water up in their hands, letting it trickle down their throats. After a while Lance got so he could swallow. Lockjaw, sitting next to him, could, too. Lance could see the painful workings of his throat.

Then Doc Grimson made them stop. They lay back and rested, in a kind of delicious agony, watching the flow and sparkle of the stream before them. Presently, they drank again, and later they sat and cupped the water up and let it run down over their faces and clothing, laughing like children, with the sheer pleasure of it.

OUT ON the desert, the dust-cloud inched nearer. It was not much more than an hour away now, and they could make out the horses and men. The animals were head-down and staggering. It looked impossible for them to endure another hour. Yet every bandit of them was in the saddle, and the watchers realized that this must be the second set of mounts their pursuers had worn out in the chase. Had they been willing to walk, to save their horses, it was more than probable that they would have caught up with their quarry hours before.

Presently, when they had drunk enough and rested, they went on. The mine, they estimated, could not be far away. They were safe now. It was improbable that any of El Lobo's men, going the roundabout trail through the hills, had gotten ahead of them.

It was after sunset, however, before a turn in the steep, winding trail Charlie Parr had picked out for them, brought them within sight of a huddle of adobe buildings and frame construction which they knew was the Bar Bullion mine.

Curiously, except for the girl, the sight brought them no elation. Into Doris Enderby's eyes there crept a light of ardor, but the others plodded on in silence. They were a-foot again, because the up-trail had been steep, and a killing weariness was on them. Lance looked at his companion's boots, cut to ribbons, as were his own by the rock and salt beds of the desert, saw their dragging footsteps and realized that they must feel as he did. The tension on his nerves once released, the anguish of thirst once relieved, his only need was sleep. He wanted to throw himself down on the trail and sleep the clock around. He had never felt so tired in his life.

Perhaps that was partly why neither he nor they showed any signs of pleasure at the sight of the mine—because it merely meant that they would have to walk so many more steps before they slept. But another and more important reason was the sense of foreboding which sprang from their lack of confidence in Bart McAllister. If anything goes wrong here, Lance told himself, we'll be helpless.

He had scarcely begun to think that when things began to happen ahead of them. An armed guard saw them and shouted excitedly, pointing. Another ran out, looked and ran back. A moment later a group of a dozen emerged, all carrying carbines, and came down the slope toward them.

Automatically, Lance reached down to assure himself of the presence of his guns and to loosen them in their holsters, but he noted that Doc and Charlie made no move towards theirs. No doubt they were right. With El Lobo behind them, and in the condition they now were, their best chance was to placate Bart McAllister and his guards at all costs. At least for the present.

In a moment they were surrounded by a shifty-eyed crew, who reminded Lance of curs who are divided between the desire to snap and an alert, cringing respect for their own skins. They all carried rifles at the ready.

One of them, evidently the leader, said to Charlie Parr: "You give us your guns," in a tone which carried a sort of hesitant insolence.

Charlie's old blue eyes blazed in quick wrath. "Who do you think you're talking to, dog?" he snapped in Spanish. "We give our guns to no man—and when you speak to us, be careful to say 'Señor!'"

The man looked abashed and furious. "It is the order—no one can come here with guns," he muttered.

"Take us to Señor McAllister, at once," Charlie commanded. "This lady is the Señorita Enderby, owner of the Bar Bullion Mine."

The guard shot an appraising glance at Doris, but there was no surprise in his eyes, and to Lance the fact was ominous.

"This way," he said, after a moment's hesitation. They followed him. The guards closed in around them.

At the door of a frame building which was evidently the mine office, the guard halted. "Señor McAllister will see the señorita alone," he said. "If the señorita will enter…" he bowed with what seemed to Lance ironic courtesy.

Doris Enderby hesitated. Lance thought that there was no anger in her expression, but some other emotion akin to excitement and anticipation. "These men don't understand," she said, after a moment. "I'd better go in and explain. Mr. McAllister will straighten everything out."

Doc Grimson started to speak but changed his mind. Charlie Parr, after a glance at him, nodded and said: "We'll wait here for you."

The girl turned and went in.

Lance became suddenly conscious that the guards had edged in closer to them. He had a vague idea that they ought to do something about that, but the leaden weight of fatigue which bore down on him prevented him from thinking about it very clearly. Suddenly, he heard Lockjaw snarl: "Keep back from me, you skunk!"

Lockjaw had turned toward one of the guards who had crowded in on him, and his hand had gone toward his gun. There was the sudden crack of steel on bone as a guard behind Lockjaw brought his rifle barrel down on the big man's head. Lance's own hand drove for his gun, but a guard flung himself at his arm and hung there, clinging desperately. Another was at his other arm.

He jerked himself suddenly back, stumbled over a rock and went down, seeing, as he did so, Doc Grimson sag to his knees under the heavy blow of a rifle butt driven at the base of his brain. Charlie Parr was struggling desperately in the grip of two guards whose strength was evidently too much for his exhausted body. Flint Maddox was on his knees, his head bloody but his hard fists driving upward at the Mexicans who piled on him.

One of Lance's arms jerked free as he fell but the other guard fell with him. He brought his knee up in a vicious drive to the Mexicans' stomach, rolled free and came to his knees. The other Mexican had clubbed his carbine and swung it now at Lance's head. Too late, he ducked. The heavy butt missed his head but drove against his shoulder with numbing force.

For the split part of a second his left arm and shoulder were paralyzed with the shock and bruising pain, but his right hand caught the rifle butt and held it. He yanked, and the Mexican came tumbling toward him. He caught the man's belt with his left hand and dragged himself to his feet, his right snapping up, with the full drive of his body as he came onto his toes. It caught the guard squarely under the chin. His head snapped back and Lance could hear the spinal column pop sickeningly. A choked gasp blew from the man's mouth before he toppled, falling, with his head lolling limply on its broken neck.

Then something landed square on Lance's head. His brain blazed with dazzling light, and then he was sinking down—down into a pit of blackness.

CHAPTER 7
FANGS OF THE WOLF

W HEN LANCE CLAYTON struggled to consciousness it was broad daylight. His shoulder was stiff and sore and his head ached. He sat up and took stock of his surrounding. The five were evidently in the mine prison, and they were not alone there. Two Yaquis shared the same large room, its floor only hard-packed earth. A window, pierced high in one wall was barred heavily with iron. In the far corner was a door. It looked heavy and it was covered with metal.

Flint Maddox was awake, staring out the window. Doc Grimson was bent against a far wall, evidently examining it to try to determine its strength. Lockjaw lay on his back with a sulky expression, staring at the ceiling. Charlie Parr, near him, was still sunk in the deep sleep of exhaustion.

At Lance's movement, Flint turned and smiled at him faintly. Flint's head was tied up in a piece of his shirt. The blue material was dark-stained where the slashed scalp had bled.

"Come over to the window, Lance," he said. "It smells better."

Lance got up and went over. This so-called jail had evidently housed a good number of Yaquis since it had been last cleaned. It was not a pleasant place.

Doc Grimson joined them. "Nice reception *we* got," Lance remarked. "But at least, this way we got away from El Lobo."

Doc Grimson looked at him queerly. "Did we?" he asked.

The question crystallized a lot of things in Lance's mind.

"You think Lobo and McAllister are together in this, Doc?" he asked.

"Well," Doc pointed out, "we seemed to be expected, didn't we? There's been something phony about the deal from the beginning. From what I hear of McAllister he's not the man to let his bullion trains be looted time after time without doing something about it. He'd have the Rurales down. He'd hire guards that could shoot. He'd make things hot for El Lobo. Why hasn't he done it? Because he and Lobo have been splitting on the deal, is my guess. Then this girl writes that she's coming down here and complicates things.

"Suppose she disappeared, kidnaped by bandits. That wouldn't be anything against McAllister, would it? The game could still go on. That's where we come into the picture. We horn in and get the girl away. El Lobo is murdering mad because we've gotten the girl away from him, and even more, maybe, because Lance hit him with his fist. That's why El Lobo crashed out into the desert after us. But, just in case, he sent word to McAllister to expect us—and McAllister did a good job of it."

"But in that case," Flint objected, "why haven't they just finished us off and been done with it?"

"I've been thinking about that," Doc answered slowly, "and I don't know. The only answer I can find is that it doesn't suit McAllister's game just at the moment. If that's the case, it means also that McAllister is the boss here and not the Mexican. In that case, we may have a chance."

"We'll have to take it in a hurry then," Lance said. "If this skunk of a superintendent is up to anything with Doris, he'll have to get rid of us. We know too much."

Doc nodded gravely. "That's why I've been trying to find a way out of this hole. We've got no time to waste."

"How's it look?"

"It's adobe, two feet through. We ought to be able to dig out in one night, if we weren't interfered with. But if McAllister's got guards that are worth their salt they'll never let us get away with it."

Lance's face was grim. "It's not only on our own account that we've got to get out of here," he said. "If a skunk like that has got his hands on Doris...."

A SMALL panel in the iron door slid back. "Get back against the wall, you dogs, if you want to eat," a voice said in Spanish.

Lockjaw came to a sitting position with a snap. "You got nothin' I'd put in my mouth, you dirty yellow flea-bitten snake," he snarled.

Doc motioned him to be quiet. "Let's see what happens here," he murmured. The guard, fortunately, did not appear to understand English, and when the five Mavericks and the two Indians had taken positions with their backs to the far wall, the door creaked back on its hinges and two men armed with rifles stepped in. They stood by the door, covering the prisoners with their weapons, while a third man came in with a large pot and an earthen water container. He put these down near the door, then the three went out.

"Not much chance to rush 'em," Lance muttered as the heavy

lock creaked and he heard the sound of the outer bar falling into place.

They discovered that the pot contained a mess of half-cooked, unsalted beans. That, and the water, was all that had been offered them. They made an attempt to eat but the beans were virtually uneatable and they contented themselves with a few disgusting mouthfuls and a drink of water all around.

The Yaquis, since the beginning had preserved an unbroken silence. When the food came, they made no attempt to go to it, holding back, evidently, in the fatalistic knowledge that they would not be allowed to eat before or with their betters. They watched, with stolid, inexpressive eyes the attempt of the white men to eat. Now, when the five abandoned the pot, they went up, still in silence and squatted down before it. Slowly, methodically, chewing hard, they attacked the beans. Within half an hour the pot was empty.

Doc watched them with the cold devils of humor beginning to dance in his eyes. "I don't think we'll be here long enough to learn that trick," he said, "but you can't ever tell."

They grouped themselves at the window and stood looking out. The company street was deserted, except for a slatternly squaw or so, the men being, no doubt, all at work in the mine. Around the corner of the jail building they could hear the laughter and talk of the guards.

Three figures came down the street, walking swiftly. In the lead, they recognized El Lobo. The bandit's face was like a thunder-cloud. As he passed the window of the jail he saw the five standing there and halted, his hands on his hips, his eyes, in the coarse pock-marked face, blazing.

"You think you have gotten away, don't you, my little gringo dogs?" he rasped. "Don't deceive yourselves. One doesn't escape the vengeance of El Lobo so easily!"

"What's the matter, amigo?" Lance asked politely. "Don't you like the desert? Do you find it a little wasteful of horses? Ah, I see, it is because you know how men will laugh when the tale goes round of how the great El Lobo could not catch the gringos!"

"Ah-h," the bandit snarled, and spat at the window.

"How'd you ever have brains enough to know we were going by the desert, anyway?" inquired Charlie Parr offensively.

The bandit looked suddenly contemptuous. "You think you can fool me, eh?" he asked, with a vainglorious air. "Ah, when you have learned to read the little things, you may set your wits against El Lobo. Do you remember that you have spilled a little wine, eh? That was not wise. You have stolen the wine bags of that poor man—very good! Maybe you want to drink a little wine, no? But then you spill the wine on the ground. So I think—ah! they are for water, those little wine-skins. And so much water—that is for the desert, no?"

"Thought so," remarked Charlie Parr gloomily.

"But it didn't do you much good, did it, my little skunk?" asked Lance. "You lost the señorita. You lost your little gringos. And now you have lost the friendship of Señor McAllister—no?"

The bandit's face purpled. "The Señor McAllister has lost

the friendship of El Lobo. He may regret it. But for the gringo curs there is still El Lobo's bullets!"

As he said the last words his hands flashed to the Colts in their ornate holsters at his thighs, and came out blazing sudden thunder. For a man nearing fifty and getting a little paunchy, it was a very fast draw. But not fast enough. When the Colts spoke the window was empty. Even Lockjaw had managed to drop out of sight.

The guards came rushing around the corner of the building. At sight of El Lobo, however, they checked.

"Not so fast, my children," the bandit advised them. "If you wish to be happy in these mountains, it is best not to set yourselves against El Lobo."

"Pardon, señor," one of the men stammered. "We—we didn't know—you...."

"And perhaps you didn't know either that I am no longer the friend of Señor McAllister? Learn it, my children—learn it now. For I am going, but in a little while I come back. It will be wise for you to be gone into some safe place before I get here." He turned on his heel and marched down the street, leaving the guards staring at him with slack jaws.

Doc Grimson whistled softly. "Trouble in the wind!" he exclaimed in a low voice. "When thieves fall out...."

"Maybe," said Flint. "Maybe McAllister is honest after all."

"Then why are we here?" asked Charlie Parr drily.

"I wish I knew what had happened to Doris," said Lance.

CHAPTER 8
THE IRON DOOR CLOSES

H E WAS soon to find out. It was not ten minutes after the incident with El Lobo when two more figures came down the street. They were Doris Enderby and McAllister. They were walking close together and talking with, apparently, the greatest friendliness!

Lance Clayton saw them first and swore softly. His exclamation brought the others to his elbow.

"Look!" Lance said bitterly. "Look, and then put some more faith in a woman!"

But the others were silent, for as the pair came nearer it became obvious that Doris was insisting on something—something to which McAllister showed resistance.

As they came opposite the jail, the girl stopped and stamped her foot, saying something in an imperious tone, the words of which they could not catch. McAllister stood looking down at her with a flushed face. He seemed not so much to be paying attention to her as to be occupied with some sudden impulse which had arisen within himself.

McAllister, they saw, was a well-built, hard-looking man of more than middle height, with a determined jaw and cold blue eyes set wide from a strong, jutting nose. Charlie Parr eyed him appraisingly. "Looks like a pretty able citizen," he observed in a low tone.

It became evident that McAllister had finally reached some sort of decision. He clipped something out to the girl which made her start back from him. It was plain that what he had said had struck her with both astonishment and the beginning of fright.

The mine superintendent allowed a thin smile to curve his hard, well-cut mouth and then took her by the arm and began to pilot her across the street.

"You want to see them, do you?" the five heard him say. "Come ahead, then, and see them." His tone was dry, ironic.

The girl, looking a little dazed, allowed herself to be led. A moment later, the iron door at the end of the room opened and the two came in. Two guards with rifles ready slipped in behind them.

Doris Enderby stood for a moment just inside the threshold taking in the details of the prison with horrified eyes. Then she took several steps toward the five Mavericks, her hands outstretched.

"Oh!" she cried, "Forgive me! I didn't know. I hadn't any idea. He told me you had been taken to the hospital—were being well cared for!"

"We've been well-taken care of, all right," Charlie Parr told her drily.

The girl whirled on McAllister, her eyes blazing with indignation. "What do you mean by such a thing?" she demanded passionately. "You know what these men have risked for me. Release them immediately. I order it!"

McAllister had leaned casually against the wall and had begun to roll a cigarette. He finished before he spoke.

"I guess you don't understand things as quick as you might,

Doris," he said, looking at her under lazy lids. "Nobody gives orders here but me."

"I expect you don't understand very well either," the girl blazed at him. "I happen to own the Bar Bullion Mine. If you've forgotten it, you'd better learn it again as quickly as possible."

"Yeah," McAllister told her, unimpressed. "You own it, but I possess it. There's a difference."

"He means," Lance Clayton cut in savagely, "that him and El Lobo possess it in partnership."

McAllister grinned a little at that. "You're a little behind the times," he replied. "That little partnership has been dissolved."

"You yellow crook!" Lance snapped. "You'd steal from your own mother wouldn't you?"

McAllister straightened up. His eyes were cold. "You've got more guts than sense," he observed, "seeing the fix you're in. Don't push me too far. I don't like to beat up prisoners, but I will if it's necessary."

The girl had been staring from one to the other in unbelieving horror.

"You mean that when El Lobo robbed the trains, it was with *his* permission?" she asked Lance.

The latter looked at the superintendent. "Why don't you answer that, McAllister?" he asked.

The superintendent looked faintly contemptuous. "I'll answer it," he said harshly. He turned to Doris. "Did you honestly think," he asked, "that I was fool enough to sit around here like a good, humble, faithful servant and turn over the proceeds of this mine to you—just because your Dad located on it? What

The two guards swung their rifles menacingly on Lance, as Doc Grimson's voice cracked out warningly.

did you ever do for it? Could you run it? Could you do anything with it, except spend the money I sent you? Don't be a little idiot. Of course I've gotten what I could out of it—and you can take it from me that I haven't finished yet."

Doris Enderby appeared not even to have heard him. At his first words she had dropped her head in her hands and before he finished she had begun to sob—little, short, gasping sobs that tore at her chest like a fit of coughing.

FOR A long moment there was silence in the room. Then Lance Clayton said between his teeth: "You think you're not through, but don't be loo sure of it. I'm not through yet. When I am, I'll have that dirty hide of yours hangin' up to scare the pole-cats away."

The girl, with an effort of will which wrenched at her entire body, forced herself to stop crying. When she looked up her face was pale and set. She stared at Bart McAllister out of eyes full of a kind of tragic wonder.

"And to think that I thought I loved you!" she said slowly. "I fell in love with you when I was just a little girl—when you scarcely knew I was alive. I've dreamed of you all these years. I'd have trusted you with anything I had—with my life. I'd have given my life for you. When I came out here, it wasn't to investigate you, but to help you—to be near you.

"Do you think I'm shameless to tell you that? I'm not. I'm just telling you what a fool a little girl's dreams will make of a grown woman. I'm telling you that because I despise you now—more, I think, than any man was ever despised before. I hate you—do you understand? I hate you, but I despise you more than I hate you. I think you're the most contemptible human being who ever lived."

McAllister laughed shortly. "I guess it's supposed to be my cue to think I've over-played my hand," he said, ironically. "But

I haven't. Do you think I'd like to have this mine that I've sweated over and sweated silver out of as a gift from a little girl? I take what *I* want. You think you hate me now—you may even try to despise me. But you'll get over that. When you wrote that you were coming down here, you were just a nuisance to me. I meant to turn you over to El Lobo and get rid of you. But these gentlemen"—he bowed ironically to the five Mavericks—"spoiled that idea. They brought you to me and I got a look at you. I know what I want when I see it, and I wanted you—on sight. That changed the play a little, and incidentally caused a slight rift between El Lobo and me. He had set his heart on you, it seems, and even more he had set his heart on playing some little games with your chivalrous friends here. I had to disagree with him.

"I'm keeping you for myself, Doris. And I'm keeping your friends alive, because I think they will help me to keep you from being stubborn. They're going to help me to make you my wife. You won't get the dear, dear husband you seem to have dreamed of, but you'll get a master, which is a better thing for a woman. You won't be coming to me and saying that I owe everything I have to you. You'll be thanking me for permitting you to share in the money I might have taken away from you altogether. That's the kind of man I am—and you're going to get to love it!"

The girl stared at him in a kind of horrified fascination but her voice when she spoke was cut like a lash. "You think I'd marry you—a *thing* like you? I'd rather die first."

"I think you'll change your mind," McAllister told her. "But be careful that I don't change mine. There are worse things than marriage."

Lance Clayton swore in a strangled voice and lunged toward the superintendent. The two guards swung their rifles towards him, menacingly. McAllister did not move. It was Doc Grimson's voice, more than the guards' rifles, which brought Lance up short. "Not that way, Lance," Doc's voice cracked out warningly.

It was just in time, for the excited Mexican fingers were already tightening on the triggers. Lance stood in his tracks, raging.

"By God, I'll cut your yellow heart out!" he swore. "If you've got the guts of half a man in that white-livered, crooked carcass of yours give me a gun and shoot it out with me. Better than that—give me fifteen minutes in a room alone with you and I'll take you apart with my fingers. Will you do it? Speak up, if you're any part of a white man at all!"

McAllister's blue eyes were glacial. He appeared entirely unmoved. "Noble—noble!" he drawled insultingly. "But it won't get you anything—not even the chance to commit suicide. You're my prize package, Clayton. I'm not killin' you for a long time, if I can help it."

"You said something about using us to help you keep Doris in line," Doc cut in, "Just what did you mean by that, McAllister."

The superintendent bent a suddenly estimating glance on him. Something in this slender man's quietness was more dangerous than Lance's fury.

"Hello!" he exclaimed, with an astonishment which was only half assumed. "Have we got somebody here that uses his head for something besides yellin' with it?"

DOC GRIMSON laughed a short little laugh that had icicles hanging from it. "You see yourself as a pretty dramatic kind of bad hombre, don't you, McAllister?" he asked. "Why don't we get down to cases? You strut your part pretty well—but enough's enough in anything."

McAllister showed no sign that the words and the cold contempt in them had pricked him. Instead, he grinned appreciatively.

"That's better," he said. "It isn't me that's been pulling the dramatics. And if you think there's any part of me that's bluff, you're not as smart as you look."

"You're a pretty good man, McAllister," Doc said, "but there isn't one of us who is not better—with a gun, or with his hands, or with his head. A crook—a man whose word isn't good, who hasn't got any loyalty or faithfulness in him—is always a fool at bottom. You're a fool, McAllister. And because you're a fool, we'll get the best of you. Now go ahead and tell us just what special, ingenious kind of hell you've cooked up for us."

McAllister spat scornfully. "That's simple. When you've lived in this filth on half-cooked beans awhile, you won't ask for any other kind of hell. But there'll be a few. You might enjoy being shackled and put to work in the mine—under a Mexican foreman who doesn't like gringos. They're maybe a little too quick with the lash, those fellows, but they get a lot of work out of the men under 'em."

"Oh, you beast!" the girl cried. "You wouldn't dare!"

McAllister disregarded her. "There are some other little pleasures I can think up for you, too," he went on. "You see, you've won Doris' loyalty pretty completely. You've gallantly risked your precious hides to save her from what she thinks is a fate worse than death. She owes you a lot. When she sees you with the skin hanging around your bones in a mass of sores...."

The girl groaned aloud. "You're—you're a kind of monster," she said. "You're something inhuman!"

McAllister laughed a little grimly. "Nonsense!" he said contemptuously. "I'm offering you the honor of being my wife. When you and the Bar Bullion are safely mine, your friends can go. When you've acknowledged me as your master, then your five friends will be free to travel. I won't be afraid of any charges they may bring. You see, unhappily, your hot-tempered friend, Clayton, killed one of my guards last night. Broke his neck while the man was in the performance of his duty. Murder is what we call that, in this country. I'm well within my rights in locking them up."

"Charges aren't what you've got to be afraid of, skunk," Lance snarled at him. I'm goin' to be jury and executioner for you, all in one."

"Doris isn't going to marry you to get us out of a jam, because we're not going to let her," Doc Grimson said quietly. "What happens to her in the meantime?"

"That depends on how I feel," McAllister answered curtly. He turned toward the door, taking the girl by the arm.

Doris Enderby snatched her arm away from him. "Don't

touch me!" she flared. "I may have to marry you to save my friends from torture, but if you ever touch me, you beast, I'll kill both myself and you!"

McAllister grinned at her. "You'll get to like it," he said amiably.

It was then that Doc Grimson acted. McAllister had moved so as to be between the five and one of the guards. Doc had been standing talking with one of his hands casually in his pocket. Now it came out, holding an ordinary pocket knife with a heavy bone handle. A poor weapon against men with rifles but the right hands may do much with small materials. Doc's right hand flashed back and forward in a swift unexpected throw. The closed knife struck the free guard full in the face. And Doc followed through in a swift, cat-like rush.

As Doc moved, Lance Clayton sprang like a flash for McAllister, his right fist snapping forward toward the Superintendent's chin. But McAllister was fast. His head moved to one side so that the blow whistled past his ear. As he ducked he brought his right fist up in a short, vicious hook which landed square on Lance's mouth, snapping his head backward.

The guard, knocked backward by the blow of the knife, still had presence of mind enough to fire. The crack of the carbine in the room sounded like the explosion of a small cannon. But Doc had run forward and a little to the side, crouching, and the bullet passed inches from its mark.

"Don't shoot! Take them!" McAllister's voice rang out in Spanish.

DOC WAS on the guard now, wresting the rifle from his

hands. Only a split second behind Doc and Lance, the others had gotten into action, Charlie Parr leaping to aid Doc, Flint and Lockjaw driving for the other guard. Lance was driving piston-blows into McAllister's face.

The Mexican, seeing his danger, had leapt aside and now, disregarding McAllister's command, or not hearing it in time, he fired. The bullet hit Lockjaw in the chest, glanced off a metal match-case and slashed along his ribs, spinning him. Flint hit the guard then in a rush so hard that they both went to the floor together.

Half a dozen other armed guards rushed in. One lammed Flint over the head with a rifle barrel. Another drove a carbine butt into Lockjaw's stomach, doubling him up. Three others jumped for Doc and Charlie, while the sixth leapt to aid McAllister, who was slugging toe-to-toe with Lance.

The superintendent gave back long enough to yell: "Not me, you fool! Get the others." The guard ran then to join the four who were struggling with Doc and Charlie. Doc had gotten the first guard's rifle free for a moment and now he brought it down on a head with cracking force. The man dropped to his knees with a groan, but at that instant the fifth guard, arriving, stuck his rifle between Doc's legs and Doc went down, two men on top of him.

A rifle butt smashed to Charlie Parr's jaw and he went down, unconscious. Doc, on the floor, fought like a wildcat, driving fists and knees. The two Mexicans on him gave way, cowed by the speed and ferocity of his blows. But that was the chance the other guard wanted. His rifle smacked down onto Doc's head, and that slender man, who moved like a cat and whose muscled arms and legs had the lightning force of driven steel pistons, went limp at last.

Lance, meanwhile, was finding an antagonist worthy of his steel. Worthy of it, but not quite a match for it. McAllister knew how to box, could hit like the kick of a mule, and could stand punishment, but under Lance's flashing, sledgehammer blows he was beginning to give ground, although the whole fight had not, so far, lasted a full minute.

Then a rifle butt drove to Lance's ribs with bone-breaking force, just under the heart, and as he halted, his arms dropping involuntarily under that killing blow, McAllister's right snapped true and hard to his unprotected jaw. He went to his knees, dropped forward on his elbows, fighting feebly to get up again despite McAllister's voice in his ears: "Don't be a fool. You're one against eight. Don't make us hurt you unnecessarily."

He fought upward again to his knees, his body writhing, his breath whistling painfully because of that blow under the heart, but his head was clear.

McAllister said calmly: "Stay where you are, Clayton, or I'll have the men bend some rifle barrels over that hard head of yours."

Lance looked at him out of eyes bloodshot with rage. "You're afraid to fight, you pole-cat," he panted. "You know you were getting licked, don't you?"

McAllister laughed shortly. "Licked? By you?" he repeated scornfully. "Why, you half-wit, you didn't have a chance to whip me!" Lance thought wonderingly, "Damned if he doesn't really think that!" Aloud he said: "Why don't you come on and fight then?"

"Why should I? What have I got to gain by cracking my knuckles on your pig head?" the superintendent asked in apparently honest surprise. "I've got you where I want you."

"Some day," Lance told him grimly, "I'm going to have you where I want you."

McAllister shrugged impatiently. "Let's get out," he said to the white-faced girl. As he turned, however, his eye fell on the guard who had shot Lockjaw. "When I say not to shoot," he snapped, "I mean not to shoot."

His fist whipped up and seemed to fairly explode in the center of the man's face. The blow drove him back in a flying arc which landed him with his head against the wall. He lay limp, as though dead.

"Get that carrion out of here," McAllister commanded, curtly.

When the other guards had obeyed, the superintendent again took Doris by the arm. "Let go," she told him passionately. "I'm staying here. Can't you see that your wild dogs have hurt them, you beast? Do you think I'm going to leave them?"

McAllister flung an arm about her, lifted her from the floor and swung her through the door. Lance Clayton rushed. The heavy iron door clanged shut in his face. McAllister's amused laughter came to him from the other side.

CHAPTER 9
BLOOD BARGAIN

HOURS DRAGGED by. They sat, for the most part, in miserable silence. Aching heads, sore muscles, exhaustion, and hunger, along with the filth and bad air, were beginning to make an impression even on the cheerfulness with which these five ordinarily met hard luck.

Lance sat looking at the two Yaquis, who preserved their habitual silence, except for an occasional stolid word or two exchanged in undertones. He considered talking to them in their own tongue, which he had acquired in his first stay in Sonora, but knowing the breed, he decided that if anything was to be learned from them, it would be best learned by overhearing them talk than by direct questioning. For that reason, he addressed them in Spanish, discovering, as he had expected, that their knowledge of that tongue was inadequate for any sort of extended conversation.

"Have you been here long?" he asked.

They stared at him stolidly for a moment, as though they had not heard him. Then one of them said: "No long. Two month, maybe."

"Why you here?"

The Indian, spread out his hands in a gesture which apparently meant "I don't know."

"The Señor McAllister is a very hard man—no?"

"Hard, yes—much beatings."

"You no like him—I no like either."

81

The Indian grinned. "You get much beating also," he said, working his fists. "Señor no like."

"Other Yaquis no like señor, also," Lance remarked, "Why Yaquis no help us get out—then we kill Señor McAllister."

At this suggestion the Indian's face became, if possible, more expressionless than ever. *"No comprendo,"* he grunted. Nor could he be made to say more.

A little later, he caught the Yaqui looking at him with a curious expression of malevolence. He did not at the time understand exactly why but he realized that he could expect no help from that quarter. The fact that the five Mavericks were enemies of McAllister made no difference. They were white men, and hence objects of dislike and suspicion.

That night, however, an incident occurred which lent another color to the Indian's unfriendliness. Lance, who was sleeping near the window, waked with the sound of guttural murmuring in his ears. Somebody was talking near him. Without changing his position, he strained his ears to catch the words and recognized, after a moment, that the talk was in Yaqui.

"...They quarrelled over the girl," was the first sentence which came to his ears. For a moment he thought they were talking about the quarrel between himself and McAllister that morning but the next words corrected him. "El Lobo will win, I think—the guards will not fight much against him."

The other voice said, "If the guards do not fight, it will not give us a good chance."

Lance realized that one of the voices came from outside the window, the other from within.

The Yaqui outside said: "Some, perhaps, will fight. El Lobo will lose many men, for the chief McAllister is a terrible man. Then, afterward, the men of the Wolf will make themselves drunk like pigs. We strike then, and, lo! none are left."

"Ah-h!" the low cry was like the snarl of an animal, and turning his head a little, Lance could see that the Indian inside had grasped the bars of the window as though to twist them apart. "May it come soon!" he said.

"Moreover," the man outside said triumphantly, "if the gringo wins, it will be the same. Death to one white man or the other— what does it matter? The tribes are ready."

His voice had risen as he spoke these last words and a guard, possibly attracted by the sound, stirred around the corner. There was instant silence and Lance saw that the Yaqui inside had withdrawn from the window. He could hear the nearly inaudible shuffle of his feet as he moved back to his sleeping position against the inner wall. A moment later a low murmur of voices from that direction told him that the Indian was retailing the news to his companion.

Lance lay still for a long time, thinking. There was no need to rouse the suspicions of the Indians by attempting to tell the others what he had heard. There was nothing to be done that night. Evidently, they were in for one of the periodic uprisings of the Indians—affairs which, he know, could be terrible in their cruelty and brutality. But evidently also, the uprising would wait on the outcome of the fight between El Lobo and the mine forces. When would that take place? Did McAllister know about it? Should Lance warn him?

IT WAS a decision very difficult to make. Everything in Lance revolted at going to the mine superintendent's aid, yet the fate of Doris would no doubt be even worse if she fell into the hands of El Lobo, and undoubtedly, a victory for the Mexican would mean immediate death for themselves. He decided he had better wake the others and make an attempt to get into touch with McAllister before morning.

But even as he thought that he became aware that the bars of the window were outlined now against a square of watery gray. Day had broken. He stood up, stretched and yawned ostentatiously, went toward the window. After a moment he walked away and managed to stumble over Doc Grimson, awakening him and apologizing in a voice that waked the others.

Charlie Parr swore at him irritably and Lockjaw emitted a groan as his first movement brought a stab of pain to the crease along his ribs.

Speaking English, in the certainty that the Yaquis would not understand, he told them what he had overheard. They agreed, after discussion, that McAllister should be told.

Lance went over to the door and banged on it to attract the attention of the guards. There was no response. He listened but could hear no movement. No doubt they were all asleep. It was a pity, he thought, that they had not tried to dig their way out that night, although what they would have done it with, he did not know. There wasn't an implement among them—even Doc's pocket knife, which had evidently been overlooked when the guards first emptied their pockets, had been lost to them in their unsuccessful attempt to rush McAllister.

He knocked again, more loudly, and when that brought no results began to kick against the door with the heel of his boot.

Silence.

He went back to the others and then, at Flint's suggestion, yelled out the window. His shout brought several curious Indians from the laborers' shacks across the way, but there was no response from the guards.

The five exchanged questioning glances. In each of their minds was the Yaqui's judgment, repeated to them by Lance, "the guards will not fight." Had they deserted already? If so, the mine, Doris, and they themselves were at the mercy of El Lobo. Trapped in here, they simply had no chance.

"If we work hard enough on these bars they might come loose," Lance suggested, without much hope.

Doc Grimson nodded. "We can take turns at it," he agreed. But Lance read the thought in his mind: "Keep them occupied. Doing something is better than idle waiting, even if the thing is hopeless." And those bars looked hopeless enough. They were nearly as thick as a man's wrist and no doubt were set deep in the adobe.

Lance took hold of one of them with both hands and pulled with all his strength. Then he pushed as hard as he could. Back and forth, he exerted his force until the cords stood out on his neck, the veins swelled on his temples and the muscles on his big shoulders rippled and bunched until it looked as though they would burst the stuff of his shirt. But when he had finished, the bar stood as before.

Stubbornly, he began again. A voice said: "It's not much use.

85

They're set almost the full depth of the wall." He looked up to find McAllister standing outside the window.

Lance's face hardened. "We've been looking for you," he said curtly.

"And I'm looking for you," the other replied. "Wait a minute and I'll be in."

He moved toward the entrance to the building and a moment later the small panel in the iron door slid back. "I can come in two ways," he said. "With a gun in my hand and you back against the wall, or on your word that you won't try anything. Take your choice."

They heard him chuckle, evidently at the expressions on their faces. The man had the gall of the devil.

Doc Grimson swore softly. "This buzzard is worth knowing!" he said, his eyes dancing with cold humor. "All right, come in. We won't try anything," he called out.

The door opened and McAllister stepped in without hesitation. "Kind of surprised that I should take your word?" he asked, grinning his hard grin. "That oughtn't to surprise you. That's the kind of hairpins you are, isn't it—full of honor and all that sort of mush?"

Doc Grimson said, "That's the kind of hairpins we are, all right. It's just kind of surprising to find a man without any honor at all who can still recognize it when he sees it."

"I've made a special study of fools," McAllister told him drily. "There are lots of different kinds of them and they all have their uses, if you know how to get at 'em. Your kind is the easiest of all."

"Yeah, there are a few things about our kind that you can count on, all right," Lance Clayton told him. "One is that I'm goin' to kill you the first half-chance I get."

"Still eatin' fire, Clayton? Still fightin' dragons for the fair? Well, I've got one for you to fight. That's why I'm here."

"The guards have run off, so you want us to help you fight El Lobo—is that it?"

"You had brains enough to figure that out, did you? I'm beginnin' to like you better and better, amigo."

DOC GRIMSON looked amused. "Do you remember the fable about the frogs who needed protection from their enemies and so asked the stork to come and be their king?"

"You think you're goin' to eat me up afterwards, do you? Wrong! I'm lettin' you out of here and givin' you guns on your word that when the fight's over you'll give up the guns again and come back to jail, just like you are now."

Charlie Parr exploded profanely. "Well, you danged, brass-gutted cockroach!"

Lockjaw sat up with a grimace of pain. "Have we really got to keep our word to this here locoed tarantula," he demanded angrily. "Let's step on him now!"

"It's a good bluff, you tinhorn skunk," said Flint Maddox, "but it won't work. You need us a lot worse than we do you."

"You're not thinkin' I guess," McAllister said calmly. "I can fight, or I can run. You don't think I've been so dumb all these years as not to have my get-away arranged. I can run and I can come back with Rurales, and everything'll be the same for me. But

87

when I get back, you won't be here. Your bones will be staked out on ant-hills."

"Why don't you just run then?" Doc Grimson asked.

"Because I don't like to give El Lobo that satisfaction, that's all. Strictly speakin' I'm not a runnin' kind of a man."

Doc Grimson said: "No can do, mister. We're not playing."

McAllister laughed shortly. "I think you will," he countered. "You're forgetting about Doris. What will happen to her when that Greaser gets her won't be much pleasanter from your point of view than what will happen to you."

Lance Clayton's face was expressionless when he said: "What's the odds? El Lobo's no worse than you are. He may be better. He's a wild man but I hear he's got some kind of a heart. I'd rather take a chance on him than on you."

McAllister grinned sardonically. "Another poker player, huh? Well, all right—make your bet. What terms do you want?"

"You give us our guns," Doc cut in indifferently, "and we'll fight your fight for you. After that we take Doris and ride. From then on, all bets are off."

McAllister's face froze. "Hell," he said, "I thought you'd show some sense. But I guess we're not gettin' anywhere. I'll be ridin'." He turned and walked toward the door.

"Wait just a minute," Lance said. "I've got a little better proposition to offer you. You let us out and after we've licked El Lobo you and me fight it out, fair, with guns or any other way you want to fight. If you live, the others here will go back to jail."

"And what if you don't happen to live through the scrap with El Lobo?"

"Then you fight Doc Grimson, or one of the rest."

McAllister turned to the others. "Do you all agree to that?" he asked, and there was a little note of wonder in his voice.

The chorus which answered him was vigorous enough to remove any doubt.

He shrugged, and his voice matched the contempt in their own as he said: "You're a lot of fools. I could take you on one by one and wipe you out. But if you want it that way, why have it. So long as I don't have to kill all of you, it's all right with me. I need some of you left for a club over Doris."

"You agree, then?" Lance asked, unable altogether to repress his eagerness.

"Yeah," McAllister said drily, looking at him with a hint of cold pity in his eyes. "I agree. Come on—let's get goin'. The greaser'll be here any minute now."

CHAPTER 10
THE WOLF ATTACKS

A S THEY stepped outside the jail, the first thing that caught Lance's eye was a signal fire far up in the hills.

"We ought to tell you," he said to McAllister, "that you've got something worse on your hands than a scrap with some greaser bad men. Your Yaquis are just waiting for you and El Lobo to cripple each other before they rise up and tromp on the party that wins."

McAllister looked contemptuous. "The Yaquis!" he snorted. "Don't worry about them. They're always talking revolt. It never comes to anything. Show the dogs a whip and they'll put their tails between their legs quick enough!"

Lance told him what he had overheard the night before. McAllister shrugged. "It doesn't mean anything. What little guts they can work up in themselves by talk will evaporate when they see what happens to the Wolf's pack."

The five Mavericks exchanged glances. They knew something about the Indian mind, and they knew what the Bar Bullion Yaquis must feel about the superintendent's treatment of them. They didn't share his confidence that nothing would happen.

Lance said curtly: "You think you know it all, McAllister, but for myself, I don't think you know enough to hog-tie a new-dropped sheep!"

"I've known, enough to run this mine for some years. I don't need any handsome young imitation outlaws to tell me what's what."

"Your time of running this mine will be over at sunset, McAllister!"

A Mexican, dressed in the nondescript uniform of the mine guards came dashing around a corner. His brown face had changed to a sort of dirty gray and his eyes were big. "El Lobo!" he shouted. "He comes! He comes!"

Behind him, hurrying and a little pale, appeared Doris Enderby. *"Adonde?"* asked McAllister of the Mexican. "Where is he now?"

"They come down the little valley—many of them. Fifty—a hundred! They come fast!" the Mexican told him, breathless.

McAllister laughed his short, harsh laugh. "That means twenty-five to forty, I guess," he said in English. "Have you see them, Doris? How many are they?" His voice, as he addressed her, had a curious note of deference in it.

Doris said coldly: "I think there must be nearly forty or fifty. I saw them through the glasses. They're a mile or more away."

The superintendent turned to the others. "We've got to move fast," he said. "Come up to the shack and get your Colts and rifles. Then we'll spread out on the ridge to the north and give the wolf pack a little surprise."

"Why didn't the fool attack at night?" Doc asked.

"Didn't you know? It's one of his superstitions. He thinks that night fighting is unlucky for him. Dates back to some early failure I think."

"Lucky for us," Charlie Parr grunted.

"Thought you said your guards had deserted," Lance remarked sardonically.

"Three of them stuck, but they're badly scared, as you can see. They think they're giving their lives for me. That dog-like loyalty's touching, isn't it?"

"You're a slimy-hearted skunk, McAllister. I don't believe there's an ounce of decency or a white square inch in your carcass."

"Don't waste any politeness on me," the superintendent told him drily, "We haven't got time for it."

They were buckling on their gunbelts by now, and the other

two loyal guards were gathering up extra ammunition to take to the ridge. Doc Grimson had looked at McAllister peculiarly when he heard about the three Mexicans who had decided to stick. Now he asked: "Have these men been with you long?"

"Five to ten years," the superintendent replied curtly.

Lance went over to Doris and put both his hands on her shoulders. "It's going to be all right, Doris," he said gently, looking down into her eyes. "You're goin' to be free and mistress of this place before sundown. All you've got to do is to stay here under cover and wait."

"I couldn't do that, Lance," the girl told him. "I've got a rifle, and I know how to use it. I'm going with you!"

There was an immediate chorus of protest at that. McAllister with the approval of the others gave her her choice between staying of her own free will or being locked up. Reluctantly, she was forced to give in.

"We'll go up to the ridge," McAllister explained. "If it gets too hot for us up there, we'll drop back under cover to that adobe there." He pointed toward a solid looking building which stood apart from the others and which had narrow slits in the walls instead of windows. "I've got it fixed up as a fort and it's hard to take."

WHEN THEY got up to the ridge, which ran across the north side of the camp at a distance of about a hundred yards from the nearest buildings, they saw that El Lobo and his men were not more than a quarter of a mile away.

Action began almost at once. The bandit crowd, a good two score strong, spread out and came up the slope at a gallop.

"Wait until they're about half-way up and then give it to them," Doc Grimson directed.

"That happens to be right, Grimson," McAllister told him curtly, "but don't try to be giving any orders around here. I'm in charge of this scrap."

Lockjaw Johnson stared at him as though he couldn't believe his ears. "Say!" he burst out in an outraged tone. "You danged, flop-eared, ignorant hunk of crow-bait! Who you think you're talkin' to? Another crack like that out of you an' I'll tromp your ears down so far folks'll take 'em for fetlocks!"

Doc Grimson smiled slightly. "Spread out, boys," he directed, as though McAllister hadn't spoken. "Lance, you take the right flank—Charlie, the left. I'll be in the center and the rest of you can take any cover you see in between."

McAllister's eyes were ice but he evidently saw that his position was too weak to be defended. He clamped his jaws tight and said no more.

They found their positions just about as the attacking Mexican reached the half-way mark. Doc Grimson's Winchester spoke first and was followed by a rattling volley from the eight other rifles. Seven saddles emptied and El Lobo himself swayed, as though he also had been hit. It was evident that one or two of the Mexican guards also knew how to handle a Winchester.

For a moment the Mexicans came on, as though the full purport of that deadly shooting had not come through to their minds, and before they hastily dismounted and took cover, three more of them dropped, either killed or badly wounded.

McAllister looked astonished and suddenly jubilant. "That's

shooting, hombres!" he called out. "It won't take long to whittle 'em down to our size at that rate!"

But it was too early to crow. The easy slope was covered with rocks and sparse brush which offered the Mexicans very good cover, once they were dismounted. And there were still thirty able rifles left. Once the initial charge was halted, the fight began in earnest.

A sudden hail of lead swept the top of the ridge. A bullet spatted against the rock behind which Doc Grimson lay. Another whined by his head. Flying splinters of stone lanced Lockjaw's face, spoiling even his rock-like aim. The Mexican guard next to Flint Maddox gave an abrupt start, shuddered all over and lay forward in a tired sort of way. His face, turned toward Flint, was a smear of blood. Lead whined and cracked around them. It sung high overhead and kicked up the dust in vicious little spurts in front of them.

The bandits were shooting fast and hard, trying to overwhelm the defense by sheer volume of fire, but a dangerous percentage of them were shooting accurately as well. For a time the defenders' fire slackened. Wise heads at this game, the five Mavericks were keeping close cover, waiting for the storm to slacken, but with eyes alert for the first sign of an advance. The bandits could not continue to waste ammunition at this rate, they knew. Not so the Mexican guards. The excitement proved too much for their judgment. They kept risking themselves to return the fire.

As one of them raised himself to get a better shot an enemy bullet ploughed down along his breastbone to enter his stomach at an angle. He jumped convulsively, raised himself to his knees and took two bullets in the chest as a hail of enemy fire drove at him.

His partner, seeing what had happened to him, cursed in fury and raised himself to return the fire. Doc Grimson yelled at him to keep under cover but the man was beside himself, consumed only with the thought of immediate vengeance. Too late, Doc called to the others to try to cover him with their fire. Before the supporting rifles began to speak, the man fell forward, struggled to fire another shot and then subsided with a groan, mortally hit.

Lance, risking himself, at the moment to check that murderous storm of lead remembered McAllister's phrase "Dog-like loyalty," and his sneer at these men's willingness to give their lives for him. "Three dead dogs," he thought with angry irony. "At least they were better men than their master. By God! I'd like to kill him three times over!"

Involuntarily he spared a glance for the superintendent, who lay nearest him. McAllister's face was a frozen mask. He was firing coldly, with machine-like precision and taking advantage of every bit of cover available to him.

A MOVEMENT in front caught Lance's eye. One of the enemy was snaking forward toward some nearer rocks. Another did the same. Two more jumped up to make a short rush across an open space to some nearer bushes. The fire in front had suddenly increased in volume. Despite the bullets humming in a vicious swarm about him Lance took careful aim and fired. One of the advancing men clapped his hands to his middle and fell forward. Beside him another dropped. The others took cover and ceased to advance.

Lance wondered who the other one of his party had been who had spotted the attempted advance. Charlie Parr, no doubt. Being on the other flank he had the same angle of vision as Lance—and old Charlie was as deadly with a rifle as he was with a six-gun.

As he fired, he saw a movement in the bushes to his right. Several men were working through them over towards his flank. He wondered what they hoped to do. The ridge on which the defenders lay was in the shape of an arc, with the points bending toward the enemy, and on his flank a bare spur ran down. They would have to cross that spur to get into position for an enfilade attack—a run of fifty or sixty yards without cover. He wondered if they were figuring on that sort of suicide.

Still, if a dozen or so of them rushed for it, some of them would get there. Then El Lobo's men could come up from the other side of the spur and deliver a flanking fire which would certainly be murderous. Ahead of him and to the right, he saw a rocky eminence, the beginning of the spur, from which position he thought he could guard better against an effort at his flank and at the same time have a clearer field of fire at the bandits in front. He'd have to cross to it in the open, but he thought the risk worth taking.

He reloaded his Winchester and filled his emptying belt from the spare ammunition beside him, then set off toward the rocks in a zigzagging run. He heard McAllister's voice calling to him angrily to come back, but a swarm of bullets had already begun to zip around him and he paid no attention.

No lead touched him, however, and within a few seconds he had flung himself, panting, behind the cover of the rocks. His sudden movement had evidently taken the enemy by surprise. They had shot too fast, and missed.

Once at his objective, however, Lance found that he had made a mistake. He was actually in a position to see better the men in front of him, but he could see nothing at the right, and in order to see anything there he would have to expose himself in full view of the flank attack if it came, and at the same time be exposed to fire from in front. He kept the position he was in, firing at the main body of the bandits and comforting himself with the fact that the movement in the bushes had apparently ceased and no attempt was being made to rush across the bare ground of the spur.

Looking down he could make out the back and legs of a bandit who no doubt had good cover from the fire in front but could not cover himself from fire from Lance's position. Lance drove a bullet into the man, feeling like a murderer as he did so.

Smoke spurted from some bushes near the dead Mexican and a bullet struck the rock an inch from Lance's forehead with a savage smack. He drove a snap shot into the bushes, realizing that the smoke had floated back and that he had probably shot high. A second spurt of smoke darted from the bushes and this time the bullet clipped the lobe of Lance's ear. At the same time, the man evidently rolled to avoid his answering shot, for the bushes moved slightly. Through a gap in them Lance caught a momentary view of a sombrero. He held his fire. Where had he seen that silver-loaded hat before? Then it came to him—El Lobo. His rifle duel was with the Wolf himself. Lance's eyes blazed. This was luck!

HE SCRUNCHED into the smallest space possible, exposing only his right cheek and eye. Even that was too much to expose, for it was evident that El Lobo could shoot. But he might miss just this one more shot, and if he did....

A rifle barrel slid through the bushes, a little to the right of the gap through which he had seen the sombrero. Something in its position told Lance that the Mexican was firing from his left shoulder. He swung his rifle in a little arc, lining the sights faster, it seemed to him, than he had ever done before, but holding with precision on a spot a little inside the rifle barrel and an inch below it. The sights had barely settled into line when he squeezed the trigger. The bushes shook. El Lobo came to his feet dropping the rifle, his hands clutching at his throat. Lance levered, lined his sights on the swaying body, but his finger would not close on the trigger. Lance couldn't bring himself to put another bullet into the Wolf, wounded or, even then, dead.

But somebody else lacked Lance's scruples. A spurt of dust leapt from El Lobo's jacket. Then another. His swaying body lurched forward and fell heavily. It was impossible to determine, in the heavy firing, who had been responsible for those two shots, but Lance guessed that it was McAllister. Lockjaw might have done it, for Lockjaw was not sensitive, but the second shot had come too fast for Lockjaw. Indeed, it was unlikely that he would have fired twice. Lockjaw had a confidence almost sublime—and almost justified—in the accuracy of his shooting.

But Lance had to admit, disgustedly, that McAllister was probably right. The death of El Lobo was more than half the battle.

These thoughts had scarcely raced through his mind when he was attracted by a slight sound behind him and to his right. He turned his head just in time to see the head and shoulders of one of El Lobo's men push up, a rifle in his hands. Desperately, Lance swung, twisting his body, cat-like, in the direction of this new threat. He shot from the hip, without aiming.

By a curious chance the bullet struck the very muzzle of the Mexican carbine—part of the lead was afterwards found clogging the bore—and twisted it from his hands. Lance levered as the man recovered and went for his knife. Another bandit appeared behind the first, and another. As the man who had lost his carbine leapt forward, his knife flashing up, Lance pulled the trigger again. This time the shot caught the man full in the stomach, but the momentum of his leap carried him forward so that he fell on Lance. As he did so he attempted feebly to complete his knife-stroke. The blade grazed Lance's cheek, drawing blood.

The men behind him, unable to shoot for fear of killing a wounded comrade, jumped in with rifles clubbed. Lance drove his knee and arm upward to rid himself of the weight on him and came to his feet ducking. His right hand flashed to his hip and flicked upward holding a Colt, but the blow from the butt he had dodged struck the barrel and knocked the six-gun from his hand. Desperately, he closed with the bandit, his right fist driving heavily to the man's solar plexus, just as four other men came over the rocks and closed in on him.

Firing along both lines stopped as though by order, as all eyes turned to the struggle on the rocks. Neither side was able to fire into the close-packed, swaying group without running the risk of hitting their own. So rapid had been the action, however, that it was a full second before Doc Grimson's voice cracked out: to him, boys! To Lance!" Doc was on his feet as he spoke, but the command came too late. McAllister was already racing toward the rocks.

"Stay still, you fools!" he flung over his shoulder, just as a small hell of fire burst out from the main bandit position. "Cover me!"

The command was so obviously sensible that Doc Grimson dropped back, with a shout to the others. A split second later the machine-like staccato rattle of his rifle led the way in helping to turn the bandit fire from McAllister.

BUT THAT fire continued fiercely. Bullets smacked into the ground before and behind the racing superintendent, whined about his head, ripped through his clothing. Lead ripped the heel from one of his boots and sent him to the ground, rolling. With the agility of an acrobat he found his feet again without a pause and raced onward.

In front of him, Lance was like a catamount surrounded by a pack of hounds. Knives flashed about him; rifle butts swung arcs in the air over his head; but the fierce rapidity of his movements was such that for a moment it looked as though he would actually get the better of the half-dozen Mexicans who were getting into each other's way in their savage attempt to kill him. His fists ripped among them like slashing hammers. Another man was down, clutching his abdomen. Still another staggered back with his nose spread out over his face like a crushed tomato. A third fought on, breathing heavily from the pain of a pair of cracked ribs. Then suddenly a crushing blow on the shin brought Lance to his knees. A rifle barrel crashed onto his left shoulder with paralyzing force. The butt of another carbine rose in the air over his head, came down with a driving force that would have certainly crushed his skull had it landed.

It did not land.

McAllister's gun spoke with a blasting roar somehow surprising amid the constant sharp cracks of the rifles. The man who was swinging the carbine stiffened suddenly. The blow still fell, but it fell crooked and without force. Then the bandit pitched forward on his face. McAllister's gun spoke again and another bandit reeled, clawing the air before he fell. The other two turned, trying to get their rifles into a position to fire, saw it was too late, and together made the mistake of trying to run for the cover of the other side of the rocks. McAllister dropped them with two more shots.

Then the bandit fire in front broke out again, searching for the two men, one was standing, with a smoking six-gun in his hand, the other still kneeling, dazed and half-paralyzed.

McAllister stooped, caught Lance under the arms and jerked

him to the shelter of the rocks, while lead tore at his clothes. Then suddenly he, too, was under cover—untouched!

Lance, wordless, wriggled painfully forward to where his rifle lay and opened fire on the gang below. McAllister seized one of the Mexican carbines and did likewise.

But the battle was already over. The bandits were withdrawing. El Lobo was dead and losses among his crew had been terrific. They drew back, firing to cover their retreat, and then suddenly broke for their horses. Of the original two score, not a dozen were able to ride away.

McAllister, alone of the crowd, continued methodically to fire until the fleeing members of the Wolf's pack were out of range.

CHAPTER 11
LIFE FOR A LIFE

L ANCE GOT to his feet and stood looking down at McAllister. His lips parted once as though he were about to say something, then closed again. The superintendent did not notice him. He continued firing after the running bandits.

Doc Grimson and the others came over. Doris Enderby came running up the slope from the rear. Lance could see the fear in her face give way to relief when she saw that all six of them were alive and almost unhurt.

McAllister quit shooting, rolled over, and sat up. "I reckon that finishes that," he remarked, hard-faced.

Lance said bitterly: "I suppose I'm supposed to thank you for savin' my life."

McAllister sneered. "If you do, you're a bigger fool than I thought you were—and that'd be a record!"

"It took a man with guts to do what you did," Lance got out, as though every syllable were about to choke him. "You didn't figger I'd be any less apt to kill you afterwards, did you?"

"You couldn't be less apt to kill me," McAllister snapped. "You're my meat, half-wit. You don't think I was going to let a lot of greasers rob me of you, do you? I'm killin' you myself, amigo, and it's going to be a pleasure."

Lance looked suddenly relieved. The others were silent. Only Doc Grimson looked at McAllister peculiarly. He looked as though he were about to say something but evidently changed his mind. The expression in his curiously luminous gray eyes was enigmatic, unreadable.

Doris Enderby had arrived in time to hear the last two sentences. Her hands went to her throat in an abrupt, breathless gesture and her eyes were big.

"You—you're not going to fight each other!" she gasped through lips gone suddenly colorless.

McAllister's eyes looked momentarily wistful as they turned toward her, but they hardened almost at once. "I'm giving your friends a chance to stay out of jail, Doris," he said, with an odd mixture of deference and arrogance in his tone. "If Clayton kills me, they go free—and you'll be free. If I kill Clayton, they go back to jail, and the situation'll be just like it was before. That's the bargain we've made."

"But—but—you can't do that. It's mad! You've all fought together. You couldn't have driven off El Lobo without them. You—you *can't* do this!"

Lance said: "Don't worry, Doris. I've stomped on more poisonous snakes than he is. I can out-draw and out-shoot him any day the sun shines, and twice when it's cloudy."

But there was panic in Doris Enderby's eyes. "You've got to

stop them," she said desperately, turning to the others. "There are four of you. You can stop this. You *must!*"

Doc Grimson shook his head and there was a hint of pity in his eyes as he said: "We gave our word, Doris. It's either that or go back to jail and leave you where you are."

"Oh! then go back! You can get out again. I—I'll marry him."

Lance said grimly: "It's no use talkin', Doris. I'm not killing him to keep out of jail. I'm killin' him to keep you from marryin' him. I'm killin' him because he even had the gall to insult you by talkin' about it."

"Maybe the idea isn't so horrible to the lady as you think it is, Clayton," McAllister put in sardonically. "Maybe she's kind of honin' to be married to a grown up man—in her heart!"

The girl said with sudden fury: "You beast! I—I hate you!"

"That's plenty!" Lance said grimly. "Let's get this little party started."

Doris had clapped her hand to her mouth as soon as the words were out of it. Now she cried hastily: "Oh, no—I—I didn't mean to say that! Please! You've *got* to give this up!"

"Your curly-headed young Galahad is too much in my way," McAllister sneered at her, in sudden anger. "What about it, Clayton—do you feel all right? Do you want to wait awhile until you're rested and in shape? I wouldn't take any pleasure in killin' you unless you thought you were at your best."

"There's nothin' the matter with my right arm," Lance told him, level-eyed. "One gun for one coyote—nobody needs more than that!"

Doc Grimson said, "You had better go back to the adobe, Doris. You don't want to see this."

The girl looked in an agony of indecision, opened her mouth

as though to make another protest, but evidently realized its uselessness and turned away. A second later, however, she turned back. "No," she said, setting her mouth firmly, though her voice sounded faint. "I'm going to stay."

She watched with hands clenched at her side while Doc Grimson stepped off ten paces, on a northerly and southerly line, so that neither man would have the advantage of the sun. But her hands came up to her throat again when he placed each man and said: "Get set, and go for your guns when I yell 'draw.'" THEY STOOD, the two of them, facing one another in the gunman's posture—weight forward on the toes, hands hanging limp and supple near the butts of their Colts. Neither looked nervous or strained, though the faces of each were grim enough. McAllister's eyes were cold and contemptuous, Lance's full of a frozen, deadly anger.

Below them, to the right, lay the valley where stretched the bodies of El Lobo's men. Already, the long shadows of late afternoon were creeping across the disorderly shapeless huddles those bodies made. To the left were the buildings of the camp, deserted now, as they had been since the bandits' presence had first been announced. Over them hung something of the same atmosphere as lay over the valley—a weighted silence, ominous and uncanny, as though death hovered there also.

The group on the ridge fell silent, motionless, waiting for the word of command which would send one more body—and maybe two—writhing into the last agony.

Doc Grimson took his time—so much time that Doris Enderby's knees shook visibly and she looked strangely white.

And still Doc waited, his eyes thoughtful. It was impossible to say whether he was mysteriously reluctant to give that word or whether he wanted to try McAllister's nerve, being sure of Lance's. But neither man so much as flickered an eye-lash and there was no sign of tension in the bodies which faced one another, relaxed but somehow immensely alert.

Then Doc Grimson's voice rang out, but what he said was not: "Draw!"

"Look out!" was what he yelled—sudden, sharp, urgent.

McAllister whirled, ducking, his hands flashing to his guns, as Lance Clayton did the same. Fast, those draws—lightning fast. Almost impossible for any but the finest eye to judge between them. But such an eye would have had to give the decision in Lance's favor.

So fast were they, that the shot which rang out from the corner of one of the buildings a split second after Doc's warning shout still hung in the air when the staccato thunder of the Colts answered it. Six Colts, for Doc Grimson had gone for his own two guns as he spoke.

The Yaqui who had fired the rifle-shot staggered backward before he crumpled up and fell on his face. Enough lead had ripped through him at one time to lift him clear of his feet!

The ridge and the ground surrounding it became all at once a bewildering hell of noise and action. Flint Maddox leapt toward Doris Enderby and swept her from her feet, tripping her, but letting her to the ground with surprising gentleness. Charlie Parr and Lockjaw were moving, weaving, their Colts blasting lead. McAllister, hatless, because the Indian's bullet had ripped through the crown of his sombrero as he ducked, lay flat on the ground, triggering his Colts with cold, machine-like precision. Lance crouched, flinging lead with deadly accuracy from both hips. Doc Grimson stood erect, his gray eyes dancing pools of light because his fierce joy in any sort of battle, the blued barrels of his six-shooters flaming and bucking in a rhythmic tattoo of death.

Between the buildings, around the corners, surged a howling mob of Yaquis—surged out and gave back as that devastating hail of lead cut, scythe-like, into their close-packed ranks. Yaquis popped up inexplicably from the valley slope of the ridge, from the rocks where Lance had fought the Mexicans, from behind the adobe building which McAllister had made into a fort. A hundred Yaquis were suddenly on all sides of them, armed with carbines, with ancient muskets, with knives, with bows and arrows, with picks and shovels and six-guns, as though they had sprung from the earth and picked up the nearest arm that lay handy.

"The fort! The fort!" McAllister yelled. "We've got to get to it!"

They formed a circle around the girl and gave back as rapidly as possible. A storm of bullets, arrows and other missiles followed them. Flint Maddox was shot through the thigh, but staggered up and kept his place. Charlie Parr took a slug through the flesh of the shoulder but kept his feet and the worn hawgleg he carried in that hand still continued to send deadly messages. Then they had gained the great open doors of the fort and were inside, while Doc Grimson tugged the nearest portal closed.

Still outside, McAllister crumpled as Yaqui lead smacked viciously against the big, solid-silver buckle of his belt and stretched him gasping on the ground. And it was the long-faced Lockjaw, who rushed back, into the fire and swung the helpless superintendent's hundred and ninety pounds onto his massive shoulder and walked to the still-open gates with him, still firing deliberately with one free hand, as easily as another man might have carried a child.

THE YAQUIS were pouring lead at them, but the lead was going wild because it took more than ordinary Indians to stand steady and fire coolly into the sudden death made by those flaming six-guns. Another second and Lockjaw, with his burden, was inside and the heavy, metal-surfaced doors swung to behind them.

Lockjaw dumped McAllister unceremoniously to the floor. "Gosh dang it!" he groaned. "I left my Winchester out there!"

The others had done the same. The range had been short and there had been no time to fool with rifles. But Lockjaw didn't notice that.

"Plenty of Winchesters in that wooden safe there," Doc said. "I saw them when the Chili guards were getting out ammunition. Break it in, Lockjaw."

McAllister sat up. "Why break it in—I've got the key," he said coolly. Then he turned to Doris who had been busy loading the hot revolvers. "It's all right, honey. I'm not hurt."

Doris, looked at him, her face pale and her eyes big with horror. At his words, she rose to her feet and an expression of cold distaste came over her face. She turned away silently.

McAllister laughed shortly and got up unsteadily. "Needn't think you can lose your man so easily as that, lovely," he went on, addressing Doris' back. The girl shook her shoulders impatiently, then her eyes fixed on Flint, who was firing methodically from one of the loopholes, a slow pool of red forming about his right foot. "Oh, *Flint!*" she cried, horrified. "You're hurt!" She ran to him. McAllister's face clouded, and he turned brusquely to the safe containing the rifles.

Flint said calmly, "It ain't much, Doris. Doc'll tend to it when we get a minute." He continued firing through the loophole.

The girl saw that his face was pale and drawn. "But you're losing too much blood!" she said. "You must let me help you."

The Indians had rushed toward the building when the door closed behind the seven, but when the firing began from the loopholes they gave back.

Doc Grimson turned away from his firing post. "Doris and I'll tend to Flint and Charlie now," he said. "You others take rifles and make these buzzards behave. I don't think they'll rush again for a minute."

Already, the long, dim room was hazy with the acrid powder fumes. Doris saw what she had not noticed before, that Charlie Parr's shirt was stained wetly red from shoulder to waist. With set, ashen lips she went to Doc's help.

McAllister dealt out rifles and ammunition. The firing outside had grown spasmodic. An occasional bullet ripped through one of the slits and smacked viciously against an opposite wall.

"If we had enough food and water we could hold these buzzards off until cows begin droppin' sheep," Lance thought.

He wondered whether they had any provisions at all, but did not want to ask for fear of alarming Doris.

Lance didn't know how many Yaquis there were, but guessed that there must be several hundred of them. He began a circuit of the loopholes, firing experimental shots to draw the enemy fire. It was as he had feared: They were surrounded on all sides. And even if they could break through the circle of besiegers, it was certain that they would be run down, lacking horses, and cut to pieces before they had gotten half a mile.

He got McAllister aside. "Have we got any food or water?" he asked.

The other gestured curtly toward the rear of the building. "Enough for maybe three days, if we're careful," he said.

Lance said bitterly: "Three days! And you planned this for a fort! Do you think these Yaquis are goin' to give up in three days?"

McAllister sneered. "No, *chiquito,*" he said sarcastically. "Why should they? They'll wait until you're starving to death or dying of thirst, then they'll walk in and cut your noble heart out."

"When it get's that bad, they won't find you alive," Lance told him significantly.

"Still snorting fire? Well, I don't know but that you've got a good idea. When we're too weak to do anything more than hold a gun, we'll continue our little shooting match. It'll be interesting to see just who has the most guts—you or me."

"The coyote strain in you will give out, McAllister. You'll have less chance than ever."

"Save it," the superintendent advised him briefly. "Night's

almost here. You'll have something more to do then than shoot off your mouth."

IT WAS true. The sun was down and the dusk was deepening rapidly. It seemed certain that the Yaquis were waiting only for darkness to renew the attack. Down in the camp streets, out of sight, the drums were beginning.

Doc Grimson located the food cache and rationed out enough for dinner. About a small adobe oven at the rear of the room they draped blankets, to shut in the light of the lantern they lighted, and built a fire over which Doris made coffee and cooked beans and bacon. The rest of the room fell into darkness.

They ate in silence, each busy with his thoughts. But circle as their minds would the five Mavericks could see no way out of their tight situation. Shut off here in the mountains, it was unlikely that anyone would learn of their plight and send help. And even if they were able to hold the Indians off during this night, the time was not far off when the water and their ammunition would be gone. Four days they might last—five, in the ultimate agony of thirst—then the end must come.

Lance privately determined that they must try to break out before then—come what might. And from the grimness in the others' mouths he guessed that they agreed with him.

As they ate the drums in the camp street beat louder, and a guttural chant took on a savage note of triumph; both rose together in a crescendo—weird, menacing, wild. Then there was silence. Doris Enderby shuddered visibly and, for the first time since they had reached the fort, her eyes were frightened. McAllister swallowed a last mouthful of beans. "I reckon we'd better get ready," he said drily. "That was the end of the war-song. They won't mourn their dead until the fight's over."

Doc glanced with a hint of concern at Flint and Charlie, who had been eating lying down and who looked pale and weary. "How about it, old friends? Think you can make it?"

Charlie Parr grinned and sat up. So did Flint. "Hell, Doc!" he said between bloodless lips. "We're all right."

A rifle spoke suddenly from the room outside, where Lance and Lockjaw were on guard.

"They're creepin' up," Lance called. And on the heels of his words Lockjaw's rifle cracked, like a period to the sentence. The attack had begun.

CHAPTER 12
LAST CHANCE GONE

D OC AND Charlie and Flint, with McAllister, leapt to their places. Luckily the attack, this time, was from three sides only, the rear of the adobe being that long bare slope up which the five Mavericks and the girl had come the day they staggered in from the desert. The slope was practically without cover for two hundred yards, and while it might easily be fired over in daylight, the Indians had evidently decided that the other sides offered greater possibilities for a night rush. That enabled the defenders to place themselves two on a side. At Doris' suggestion, she kept watch at the rear, to avoid a possible surprise attack.

The night was moonless but the glimmer of the southwestern stars made a vague light in which darker blotches against the earth showed from time to time, moving. Lance Clayton fired at one of these and cursed as he saw it shift rapidly to the shelter of a nearby rock. It was tricky light to shoot by—impossible to line his sights.

The Yaquis began a rattling fire from the background to cover the advance of the Indians who were crawling up through the darkness. Orange flashes stabbed the night and the smack of lead on the wall outside the loophole told Lance that the bullets were coming too close for comfort. It was inevitable that sooner or later some of the flying lead would find the slit in the wall—and the man behind it.

It was useless, though, to fire at the flashes. So Lance concentrated his attention on picking off those crawling forms. They were closer now. It was still hard to hit them, for they took advantage of every bit of cover, appearing, disappearing, blending with the ground, like so many dark phantoms. He sharpened every faculty for the task of locating the silent, crawling blotches before him. They had to discourage the advance before the Yaquis got close enough for a rush. Once they got up the walls of the building....

McAllister's voice came. "Watch for any of them that seem to be carrying anything. There's dynamite in the powder house, and they know how to use it!"

Lance could hear Doris' soft gasp behind him when she heard that. A form showed distinctly, in a running crouch. He waited until it paused and then squeezed trigger. The form became suddenly more distinct, taller, with its arms showing vaguely against the skyline. Then it crumpled, hit the ground with a thud.

The blotches began to move faster; they showed more distinctly but were harder to hit. Lance saw that there were more of them than he had suspected. In the darkness a good half of them had managed to come up unperceived. He levered his Winchester so fast now that the barrel burned his hand when he stopped to reload. Still they came on, with a rush and a sudden, hair-raising chorus of war-whoops. Lance dropped his rifle and drove for his six-gun.

The feel of the guns was enough to let him sling death with almost unfailing accuracy. Dark, rushing forms crumpled up as the guns blazed, but always there was a new one to take its place.

The fire from the rear had ceased now, but the attacking party had begun to shoot. Wild shooting, running through the dark— yet the lead smacked close around the loophole. Dimly, Lance was aware that a bullet had whined over his head. Another grazed his cheek. His Colts clicked on empty chambers.

Swearing softly, he stepped aside and began to reload, fingers swift and sure from belt to chamber in the dark. When he stepped back something black blotted out the starlight at the firing slit and a carbine belched fire into his face. Then his right-hand Colt roared. The breath went out of the Yaqui in a quick, grunt and he dropped out of sight.

Another was behind him. Lance's left gun dropped the half-naked body, clawing, falling forward. Swiftly, blastingly, in a continuous, staccato thunder, his guns cleared the arc in front of him.

Then light flared in his face, with the momentary vision of a hand behind it and he leapt backward and sidewise. A little too late! The ball of burning pitch, thrown from one of the blind spots at the sides of the loophole, caught him on the shoulder, burning his cheek and setting fire to his shirt.

IT WAS characteristic of him that he shouldered his guns, instead of dropping them, in order to beat out the blaze on his chest. Then, with his bandanna to cover his hands, he stooped swiftly and in one lightning movement he picked up the flaming pitch-ball and tossed it back through the loophole. As he did so, more pitch came in from the other side and Lockjaw picked it up with his bare hands, cursing blasphemously. The room was full of suffocating fumes.

The pitch he had returned through the firing slit landed on the ground some yards away where it blazed fiercely, lighting up all that side of the building. Lance could hear the sudden *"bam! bam! bam!"* of Flint's guns at his side as the light picked out his targets. Outside the night was full of frenzied groans and yells of pain. And then out of the corner of his eye he caught a sight which froze the blood in his veins. Two Indians were running forward, stooping, carrying a wooden box—rushing for the blind spot at the right of his loophole. Dynamite!

His mind yanked suddenly like a buzz-saw which hits a knot and then races forward. They were not more than twenty yards away. What would happen if that dynamite went off now? He did not wait to think. He only knew they mustn't get closer—

that every lost foot was precious. Both his guns spoke at once, driving flaming lead, not at the Yaquis but at their burden!

The earth and the skies opened. A blinding flame split the night asunder. Sound—enormous, ear-shattering, brain-shaking—blasted outward and upward to the stars. A wind of incredible violence shook the stout adobe building as frozen bush shakes in a storm. Plaster rained down from the walls. Near the roof a shower of adobe bricks tumbled inward as a section of the wall gave way.

Lance picked himself up from the floor where he had been knocked by the terrific gust. He felt dazed. About him was silence, inside and out. The silence of death—utter and complete.

Lance leaned against the wall at the side of his slit and began to laugh, hysterically. Outside a chorus of frightened yelps began from those Yaquis who had been far enough away to escape the violent death of the explosion. The yelps diminished in the distance, died away. For that time, at least, the battle was over.

They relighted the lamp, which had been blown out, and took stock of their injuries. Flint Maddox had been knocked back from his loophole, the back of his head had struck on a wooden bench and he was unconscious. Charlie Parr, at the loophole opposite had been thrown against the wall and the wound in his shoulder re-opened. Lockjaw's forehead streamed with blood from where it had collided with the rough adobe of the interior. Nobody else was hurt except Doris, who, during the fight, had been struck in the back by a ricocheting bullet. The bullet had glanced off her ribs but had made a painful wound.

"Here!" McAllister commanded roughly, trying to cover the concern he apparently felt…. "Get that blouse off of you and let's have a look at that!"

He caught her by the shoulder as he spoke, and make to rip away the light stuff where it was already torn over the wound.

"Take your hand off of me!" the girl cried with surprising violence. "Don't you dare touch me!"

Doc Grimson was busy working over Flint, so Lance stepped up and said gently: "Let me look at it, Doris."

McAllister stood with clenched fists, confronting him. His eyes were no longer cold. They were full of sudden, hot fury. Lance stared him down, level-eyed. "Out of my way, McAllister," he said in an even voice. "Unless you want me to knock you out of it."

For a split second, the other man hesitated. Then the girl said, "Thank you, Lance," in a warm voice. "Don't hit him—it isn't worth it."

Surprisingly, the anger died out of McAllister's eyes. For a moment his face went black and sullen, then he turned on his heel and went out of the blanketed enclosure. The droop of his shoulders looked somehow hopeless as the curtain dropped behind him. The girl watched him go with a small enigmatic smile of satisfaction plucking at her lips, and her eyes held an expression which somehow puzzled Lance.

"Say, what the hell happened anyway?" Lockjaw demanded, and added, to Doris, "Excuse me, ma'am."

Lance told him how he had exploded the dynamite. "At that, it was plenty close, I reckon," he finished.

119

"Close?" bawled Lockjaw. "Hombre! Next time you go to shootin' up dynamite, gimme a word of warnin'. There won't be the difference of a frawg's hair betwixt me and the North Pole before you can fan a six-gun!"

FROM OUTSIDE, at a distance, came a hail, then McAllister's voice answered in Yaqui. There followed a parley, wordy on the part of the Indian, brief and incisive on the part of the superintendent. "That was the chief skunk talking," McAllister explained. "He offered us safety if we would surrender—said they had no wish to kill us but would be forced to if we resisted any longer."

Doc Grimson laughed softly. "Kind of late thinkin' about it, wasn't he?"

"That's Injun for you!" Charlie Parr exclaimed. "They got minds like children and hearts poisonous as a gilla monster!"

Lockjaw said: "The danged coyote! What'd you tell him?"

"I told him," McAllister answered drily, "that we had food and cartridges for a month, that help was on its way, and that he'd better surrender—that if he didn't every other man would be killed and those who were not killed would get a hundred lashes apiece."

"Think the bluff did any good?" Charlie Parr asked.

"None whatever," McAllister said.

Doc Grimson laughed again. "I expect that about sizes it up," he said. "What do you think—will they attack again?"

"Not until they figure we're weak or off guard."

"They'll try at least once more before they sit down to starve us out," said Lance, who knew more about the Yaquis than

McAllister did. "But they'll wait a day or so, and then try to creep up early in the morning, just before dawn. That's for a general attack; but you can count on plenty of nasty little tricks before then."

Doris Enderby said in a suddenly shaken voice: "But what are we going to do? Do you mean that they will really starve us to death? Isn't there something we can do?"

An uncomfortable silence greeted her question for a moment. Then Lance said swiftly: "We'll find something to do, Doris, don't worry."

"That right," Doc Grimson agreed. "There's always something to do."

McAllister's harsh, cold laugh broke in on them. "The Never-say-die Boys!" he sneered. "You're up against a stone wall—and you know it!"

Lance said hotly, "You skunk! You're up against the same wall and you know even less to do about it than anybody else!"

"Yeah?" McAllister's tone was curious. "Don't worry about me. You're apt to find that I can take care of myself."

They fell silent after that, unimpressed by the superintendent's boast but too deeply conscious of the hopelessness of their position to wish to talk any longer.

It was decided that Lance and McAllister and Doc and Lockjaw would stand guard, two and two, leaving Flint and Charlie to sleep uninterruptedly. Flint had regained consciousness, but he was not yet in a condition to stand a vigil.

It fell to the lot of Doc Grimson and McAllister to take the first tour of duty and the others stretched themselves out to get some rest.

Lance Clayton, however, did not fall into the instant sleep which was his habit. He felt troubled about Doris Enderby—troubled by something in her attitude which he could not put his finger on—troubled also because he felt their responsibility toward her. Nor could he get Bart McAllister out of his mind. He hated McAllister and knew that he must eventually be killed for Doris' sake; yet, curiously, when his emotions were not being whipped up by actual contact with the superintendent he found his hatred cooling off. It could not be denied that McAllister had shown himself a man that day. Hard, he certainly was and apparently without either conscience or decency, but he had flawless courage—he was a fighter from the word go—and that was a thing that Lance could no more help respecting than he could forebear to breathe. It came to him suddenly that it was a shame that he had to kill McAllister. If the man had even a vestige of decency, it would not be necessary.... But there it was—he had not even that vestige. Even after fighting shoulder-to-shoulder with them, McAllister was capable of betraying them without a qualm.

A faint scuffling noise at the rear of the room attracted Lance's attention then and when he had dismissed it as unimportant, his thoughts turned again to Doris. In some way she was not being quite open and candid. What thing or thought was she trying to conceal? He gave it up, after a little, deciding simply that even if McAllister showed more virtues than he had thus far, he would still have to be killed on Doris' account.

He had the grace to smile at himself after that…. It wasn't likely that McAllister would ever again have the chance to harm Doris Enderby. McAllister and all the rest of them would be very dead before very long.

DOC GRIMSON'S voice came out of the darkness. "McAllister?" he called, in an odd, questioning tone. There was no answer. Doc repeated the superintendent's name more sharply. Still McAllister did not answer.

Lance sat up. McAllister was supposed to be on guard. Had the fool gone to sleep? He heard Doc moving around the room and got up and joined him. Together, they searched, but there was no sign of the man they sought.

"Kind of funny," Doc said, puzzled. "He was on his feet and seemed wide enough awake a few minutes ago."

Charlie Parr came out of the relaxed, light slumber which years of danger had taught him. "What's wrong?" he asked.

"Can't locate McAllister," Doc told him. "He was here a minute ago."

"There's only two ways out," Charlie Parr said, "front and back. If he isn't here he must have gone out one or the other of them."

"They're both bolted on the inside," Doc told him. "Besides, I don't think he could have gotten out either without my hearing him."

Lance remembered something. "Wait a minute," he said, "until I get the lantern—we'll have to risk some light."

With the lantern turned low he walked to the rear of the room. "Heard a funny sound back here, a while back," he explained, examining the walls, ceiling and floor by the dim light. Suddenly he gave an exclamation and bent over. The floor of the building was made of neatly fitted boards here and his eye had fallen on a fine line which made a square in the floor—a trap door! A rug had formerly covered it, but the rug had been swept aside and not replaced. It was evident that McAllister had gone down through the trap and had not come up.

"What's that skunk up to now?" Lance muttered, as he worked the trap open.

Flint, Lockjaw and Doris waked up and demanded explanations. Doc Grimson told them briefly what had happened. Then the trap door swung upward under Lance's fingers, revealing a flight of crude steps which led down into darkness.

Lance led the way down them with the lantern, the rest following, except Charlie Parr and Flint, who remained on guard. As they went down there came up to them from the darkness below a snuffling and stomping of a horse.

At the foot of the steps Lance held the lantern high to show a circular chamber which was evidently formed by part of an abandoned shaft of the mine. A couple of crude stalls had been fitted up there and in one of them was a horse.

The other stall showed signs of recent occupancy, but the animal which had evidently been there was gone—!

From this underground stable the shaft led off into the darkness again. Lance followed it but within fifteen or twenty yards was stopped by a heavy door. And the door was locked.

Lance cursed viciously under his breath. Doc Grimson was silent. He looked somehow profoundly astonished.

"What does it mean?" the girl cried. "Has he gone off and left us?"

Lance ground his teeth. "The skunk!" he got out, his features working with anger. "That's just what he's done! Run out on us—like the yellow coyote he is!"

Doris was white, with a kind of unbelieving horror in her eyes. "But—but it's impossible!" she burst out. "That would be too mean. There isn't anybody who would do that!"

"Nobody but him," Lance amended savagely. "By God, I had a hunch I ought to have killed him without waitin'!"

Doc Grimson said thoughtfully: "He must have had the horses waiting here for him and Doris. You remember he said when he talked to us in jail that they could escape if they wanted to?"

"Yeah," Lance agreed. "Then when he got in a tight and couldn't take Doris with him, he pulled out on us—like the crawlin' snake he is!"

"But—but why did he lock the door?" the girl stammered. "He could at least have let us have a chance to get away too!"

"That's what I wonder," said Doc.

"I'll tell you why," Lance gritted. "It's because he saw he hadn't any chance with Doris. He was sore. There were only two horses—not enough for all of us, and I reckon this secret way out wouldn't be much good in these circumstances if you was on foot. He wouldn't take the chance of riskin' his yellow hide, and he knew Doris wouldn't sneak out with him alone. He knew she hated him. He saw it tonight. So he hit the breeze and locked us in to die. That's his revenge—a white-livered murderer's revenge."

Doc Grimson shrugged his shoulders. "I guess you're right, Lance. I had got to thinkin' for a while that…. But I reckon varmints of his type are—" He broke off, without finishing.

Lockjaw said: "The danged tarantula! Let's get that door down and go kill him. He can't be far."

Doc Grimson stepped to the door and examined it closely. It was of heavy oak, with an iron bar hanging down from one side and a heavy lock which was, however, unlocked. The door was nonetheless fast and resisted all efforts to open it. Evidently a bar similar to the one on the inside held it in place on the outside.

LOCKJAW SAID: "Let me at it!" and stepping back, flung himself against it. The door never even quivered. Lockjaw backed away still farther and then ran against it full force. The impact was enough to break an ordinary shoulder, but it had no visible effect on the door.

Lance said: "It's no use. We'll have to find something to break it down with."

"I've just been thinking," Doc said soberly. "I can't remember a single thing in this building which might help us to break through it."

"There must be something," Lance protested stubbornly, but in his heart he knew he was probably wrong, for Doc Grimson had the trick of noticing things. If he said there was nothing there to help them, it was pretty likely to be so. This case was no exception, for a search of the shaft and the room above revealed nothing more useful than a table knife. Lance took it, thinking that, in time, he might be able to hack through it.

"Wait a minute," Lockjaw said, when they had come back to the door. "I'll show you a trick or two." He pulled his six-gun and sent half a dozen shots hammering into the oak. They formed a close group but they did not go through. The bullets remained imbedded in the wood.

Doc Grimson shook his head. "You'll just make the door stronger that way, Lockjaw," he said, smiling faintly.

Lance swore softly. "Listen," he said. "If McAllister could get away through this secret passage, we can, too. We've *got* to get that door down."

"We might try burning through it," Doc suggested, doubtfully. "There's kerosene upstairs."

"That's what I call an idea!" applauded Lance enthusiastically. "We'll do it."

He jumped for the stairs and in a moment was back with the kerosene. They got some straw from the stalls and heaped it at the foot of the door, soaking it and, as far as possible, the wood, with the oil. The straw burned fiercely and the oak of the door caught also, but within five minutes the shaft was so full of smoke as to be untenable. Gasping for breath they made their way to the stairs, where they found themselves confronted with a choking and terrified horse, who was making desperate efforts to break his halter.

"We'll either have to put out the fire or get this horse up in to the upper room," Doc Grimson said.

"He'd never get through the trap, even if we could get him up the steps," Lance pointed out.

It was a quandary. Aside from their humane reluctance to sacrifice the horse, the animal might prove to be the only chance of getting one or more of them to safety.

Lockjaw solved the difficulty with one of the simple, direct inspirations which sometimes came to his slow mind. He walked up nearly to the top of the steps, put his hands on the flooring and shoved. The great muscles of his shoulders leapt into knotted profile, the cords on his neck stood out, his big, barrel chest heaved and the flooring gave, cracked upward. Lance sprang to his help and within a few minutes they had cleared enough of a space to get the horse through. They blind-folded the frantic animal and with infinite difficulty got him into the upper room. Just in time, for the smoke was pouring now up the stairs as through a chimney and the adobe was so full of it that it was necessary to open the doors.

When the smoke from below began to diminish, Lance wetted his neckerchief and, with it tied around his nose and mouth, risked a dash down into the shaft. A few moments later he was back.

"Part of the oak burned through," Lance said, with a note of final hopelessness in his voice. "There's cast-iron on the other side—at least half an inch thick. I don't reckon there's any chance of getting through it."

Silence greeted that statement—the silence of people who have seen hope and had it taken away from them. Only Doris

Enderby made a sound. She sobbed once, and then was quiet again.

A rifle flamed in the night outside and a bullet spatted against the wall near the open door. Evidently the Yaqui guards had sensed that it was open. It was as though they had sensed, too, that this was the moment to put a final end to any hope they might still have of escape.

CHAPTER 13
KILLER'S QUEST

LANCE SWUNG the door to, and stood with his back against it. "Look here," he said, and there was a new, steel-like note of determination in his voice. "What's the nearest place we can get help from?"

"Aguas Frescas," Charlie Parr said.

"What's the nearest way to get to it?" For a moment Charlie did not reply, then he said slowly: "There's a way through the mountains, and there's another way—" he hesitated—"through the desert!"

For a full second nobody spoke, then Lance drew his breath in and said in a level voice: "It's nearly dawn—I reckon I wouldn't make it through the mountains. I'll take the desert way."

"Lance! You're not thinking of trying to ride out of here? Why—why it's suicide!" It was Doris who spoke.

Doc Grimson took him aside. "Look here, Lance," he said. "There's a chance in a hundred that a man could break through—and another chance that he could make it across the desert. So

129

I reckon your idea has got to be tried. But—you and Lockjaw and me will have to draw lots for it."

Lance shook his head. "I'm the youngest, and it's my idea. I'm goin'. It's no worse than stayin' here, anyhow."

Doc shook his head doubtfully. "There's always some chance for us as long as we stay here," he pointed out. "The Yaquis may give up. Help might come, somehow. We might—all five of us—manage to break through some night. But what you're about to do…." He did not finish. It was pretty plain to everybody that a lone man wouldn't have much chance to pass the cordon, and that he'd be pretty surely run down if he did. Nobody could beat the Indians and their ponies for desert travel.

But Lance set his jaw and said: "No. I'm goin'."

Charlie showed him the map of the country and sketched his way to Aguas Frescas, where there was a station of Rurales. The route led across a shorter arm of the desert than that which they had traversed coming from Querida, but there were, so far as Charlie knew, no water holes, and—what was in all their minds—there was but little water to take with him unless he got a chance to stop for some on his way to the desert…. But that was extremely unlikely, with the Yaqui pursuit hot on his heels.

He filled one canteen from the common supply, refusing more. And indeed, it was obvious to everybody that if he took much more they would have little chance of lasting out the several days it might take to get help to them. For it was found that McAllister had helped himself generously!

Lance saddled the animal and led him to the back door. "So

long, Doris; so long, boys," he said quietly. "I ought to be back in a few days."

They answered him in voices as quiet as his own, but with something poignant in their quality. They knew how good a chance there was that this was not merely "so long" but "good-bye."

Lance opened the door, led the animal quietly outside and in a second was in the saddle. There was a sudden movement in the shadows at one side and a guttural voice said something questioningly. He did not wait to find out whether or not he had been seen. He set sudden steel to the horse's flanks and shoved him into a headlong gallop, down the slope, into the darkness.

Shouts came to him faintly over the thunder of the racing hoofs and then, around him, ahead of him, the darkness burst into fierce flashes. Lead whistled about his head, whined ahead of him, zipped into the ground at the horse's flying feet. He did not draw his guns and fire in return. It was nearly useless and the flash of his guns would have made him a better target. He dimply lay alongside his mount's neck and prayed that none of the questing lead would find the quivering flesh which carried him.

THE FIRING from the rear and sides slackened a little after the first few thundering seconds but that in front increased. The bullets began to crack uncomfortably close to his ears. But the animal he was riding was evidently a fine piece of horseflesh. Under Lance's urging spurs he thundered through the darkness at a terrific pace. The flashes rushed forward at him, were on him! He saw two dark forms rise up in the dark ahead of him, one on either side.

His hand flashed to his right gun, came up spitting yellow thunder. The form on his right threw up its hands, fell forward. Lance's gun crossed like a flash to the other side, his thumb released the hammer. The crack of a carbine mingled with the roar of the Colt. Flame singed his face. Something hot brushed his ear. He had a momentary glimpse of the Yaqui sinking to his knees, with the rifle falling from his hands, and then he was past.

His horse's hoofs clattered suddenly on rock, slipped, checked their racing pace. The descent had begun.

Lance holstered his gun. He would need all his horsemanship from now on. Behind him he could hear excited yells and knew the Indians must be rushing for their ponies. He would have to take a dangerously fast pace down the slopes and ravines that led to the desert—if his horse broke a leg, he wouldn't have a chance. Dawn must not, in fact, find him anywhere in those hills. There would be signal fires with the first light. He could scarcely hope to avoid being cut off by the Yaquis, who knew every inch of the hills as he knew the palm of his hand.

He pushed on through the dark, careful enough to avoid disaster but rating his animal along at the fastest pace the terrain would allow.

Behind him, now, he heard the faint clatter of the hoofs of many ponies. He wondered if the sounds of his own progress were as audible. No doubt they were, for his own animal was shod and the Yaqui ponies probably were not. He angled down into a ravine and struck a sand bottom. If he could keep to that his progress would be noiseless enough.

Presently he heard the Indians pause, as though at a loss. Then they scattered and dimming sound of the hoofs told him that they were spreading out. One party, however, came on, directly toward him. He had an impulse to push his mount into a gallop but restrained it. Even in the sand the pound of the hoofs might be audible. He held to a walk, his nerves crisping and the sweat beginning to come out cold on his forehead.

The sand under his horse's hoofs suddenly got deeper. A breath, furnace-like, which had for him a terrible familiarity, came up from in front. He was on the rim of the desert. The real ordeal was about to begin!

Even the animal under him checked suddenly as that breath came to his nostrils. He had carried him willingly at a breakneck pace through the dark, against the rattling threat of the guns, but he had no heart for the desert. It came to Lance to wonder if the horse might have a premonition of his fate. There was not enough water for two of them. He was going to have to ride his horse to death and then go ahead on foot, and his heart was heavy in him at the thought.

The remaining hours of that night passed in a dreary monotony of dust and heat, but they passed all too quickly. Day came and added the brazen hammers of the sun to his discomfort. The sudden, fierce heat of the low morning sun had something ominous and frightened in it.

He rode glancing back over his shoulder. There was no sign of pursuit for the moment. No doubt the Yaquis were going about their preparations without hurry, fairly certain of being able to overtake him in the end.

It was after one of the backward glances, when his eyes returned to scan the horizon ahead, that Lance's heart jumped suddenly. In the distance, perhaps two hours' ride ahead of him, was a slender column of dust!

HIS FIRST thought was that some of the Indians had managed to cut him off, but then he realized that that dust could be made only by one horseman. Immediately his mind leapt to McAllister. He, too, had taken the desert trail! Of course! He would know enough not to risk hills swarming with Yaquis. The desert was in one safe way of escape. Only he, unlike Lance, had been able to leave the mine unseen, and so was able to count on not beings pursued.

Hatred and triumph flamed up in Lance and involuntary he drove his spurs into his horse's flanks. The animal leapt into a gallop. Lance laughed aloud. McAllister was exactly on his route. He could kill him and then go on to get help.

Then he sobered and pulled his mount back into a walk. He mustn't let his emotions run away with him and spoil everything. There was no need to hurry. In the end, he would come up with his prey. The certainty of it was in him like a sure premonition. He would overtake McAllister. It wasn't possible for him to fail!

He settled down to the work, bringing all his wits now to bear on the problem of getting the utmost in speed and endurance out of his mount. He did not know how much water McAllister had, but he assumed that since the superintendent had been able to get away unnoticed he had had time to get a full supply. That gave him an advantage over Lance—McAllister would be able to water his horse as well as keep up his own strength. Well, Lance would show him how fast you had to travel to escape a just death! Horse or no horse, water or no water, he would come up with him!

The day which followed showed a triumphant, though unwitnessed exhibition of horsemanship. Lance knew horses—but not even he had ever managed to get so much out of a mount. Walk and trot, rest and swab out mouth and nostrils, letting a few precious drops of the water trickle down the animal's throat, then on again. He found that he could gain time by riding at a walk and running beside the horse when the animal trotted. But his mouth began to get horribly dry and his nostrils became painfully inflamed from the swift passage of the dry, hot air.

Before the day was over the thirst had begun—the desert thirst which is not only of the throat and the body but of the brain. It frightened him to have it begin so soon. But the column of dust in front was nearer now—a full hour nearer, he judged. That was worth everything.

At sunset he halted and ate cold food, and after he had drunk and given a few drops to the horse the water in the canteen was very low. When he thought that the horse was rested enough, he pushed on again. But this time, in the late evening light, he noticed a dust-cloud behind him.

The Yaquis! He had forgotten all about them!

The Indians, however, no longer worried him. That cloud of dust was half a day's travel away. If they thought they could catch up with him, they were a good deal mistaken. They had trusted too much to preparation, fresh ponies and plenty of water. He'd beat them, and he'd catch McAllister—he'd beat the desert itself!

He shook his fist suddenly at the expanse before him and around him. "I'll beat you, too—damn you!" he yelled in a sudden frenzy.

But the desert—gray, dry, old with an age beyond computing—made no reply. It stretched before him, flat, endless, silent in the vast cruelty of its indifference—waiting.

Night came, and that peculiar blast of upthrown heat which the first darkness seems to draw out of the dry lands. The hours passed. The horse began to get so leg-weary that it stumbled frequently. Lance dismounted and walked holding on to the stirrup. His feet were blistered and bleeding. The sole of one boot had come off entirely. It was the same pair with which he had crossed this stretch of hell before....

He stumbled on at the side of his horse. After a while, he mounted again, and later still, found himself walking again, without the memory of dismounting. He supposed that some stumble of the animal had warned him that it could no longer carry his weight.

Dawn came. He mounted and rode looking forward, eagerly—anxious for the first glimpse of dust which would tell him whether or not he had gained on the dim cloud ahead of him. HE DROVE forward, slogging it steadily. From time to time, he trotted a little. It was when he trotted that he gained on the man ahead, for a man will walk even with a horse, but a trotting man can gain on a walking horse. That was what Lance knew—for the moment it was all he knew. He had no thought for anything, not even the new, brilliant, blinding hammers of the sun, not the Yaquis behind him, nor the help that might lie somewhere—ahead. There was no time to think of anything except the fact that a trotting man can come up with a trotting horse—if the man can keep trotting!

He did not try to keep trotting. It was an agony almost unendurable to keep moving one bleeding foot after another. That was walking. When it came to trotting, the thing was clearly impossible. Nobody could do it.

Yet anyone who had followed those bloody tracks in the sand would have known that the man who made them was trotting part of the time. Somehow the ruthless will drove the muscles forward, sending the tortured feet pounding forward—faster, faster—until the will broke a little and the slogging, blood-spurting walk began again.

He was gaining. Three-fifths of a mile now—a quarter! Then something happened that stopped the heart in his breast and set his brain reeling in sudden blackness of despair. The horse ahead began to trot also!

No reason why that should have surprised him. Yet it did. He had come to think of that horse as an animal with only one gait. It was impossible that he should trot. It brought him to a staggering, gasping halt. And as soon as he was halted, he went to his knees, unable to stand.

He had lost! Just as he had been about to win, he had lost! Somehow, from the depths of his parched and fevered body, his eyes produced tears. Hot, blinding tears of rage and frustration, which ran saltily down his cheeks and dripped, burning, in the cracks of his split lips.

Then he was up on his feet again, slogging forward, at a walk now. The horse could not trot forever. Somehow, sometime, he would wear him down.

He went on, dogged—each step like a day's labor achieved. But he went on. And sooner than he had expected, the horse stopped trotting. He did not merely stop trotting. He went down on his knees, as Lance's horse had done, and he did not get up.

A hoarse shout broke from Lance's lips—a kind of dreadful croak. Now! Now, let McAllister see who was the better man!

He drove on, quickening his pace—less tired all of a sudden. McAllister stood beside his fallen mount a moment, looking back at the figure which followed behind him. Then he, too, turned and walked ahead.

Lance went on. The light seemed less bright to him now—the red haze was before his eyes—and the torture of thirst was on him. His brain, the very shrivelled core with the flame which consumed him, cried out dreadfully for water. Still he went on. Sometimes McAllister was visible to him, sometimes he disappeared in the heat haze or behind some fold in the ground. At these latter times, Lance quickened his pace, frantic, for fear that he had lost him for good.

He fixed his eyes on the figure ahead of him. Nothing mattered beside his need to kill that creature who crawled through the dust and haze ahead of him. He forgot, almost, that anything else depended on him—forgot that five lives hung on his. Somehow he would win through. But just at the moment, only one thing mattered—to kill the traitor!

And he was gaining! Slowly, inevitably, like the march of death itself, he was creeping up. He fought to get the rapid breath through his thickened throat, in which the tongue lay, motionless, like some great, dry, swollen slug. He fought to drive the slogging pistons of his legs faster and faster. His sombrero weighed on his head like ton of lead. Its band tightened around his forehead as a heated iron tire binds a wagon wheel. Impatiently, he tore it off and tossed it aside.

THE SUN beat with a murderous hammer on his bare head but he scarcely knew, for the twin fires of thirst and hate burned in him with a violence to make outside heat seem harmless. His shirt and undershirt began to chafe the gritty skin of his body unbearably. He tore them off and left them on the sand behind him.

He went on. Once, he dropped to his knees and began to digging for water which he heard running in a cool, bubbling stream just under the surface of the sand, but he remembered that he had done that on another occasion and that there was no water there.

After what seemed endless time, while he slogged forward with down-bent head to avoid seeing the mirages, he looked up and there, through the red haze, was McAllister—not two hundred yards away.

Lance gave a great cry, which did not somehow emerge from his throat, and drew his guns. Maybe if he shot, McAllister

139

would stop and fight. The Colt in his right hand bellowed surprisingly loud in that sun-stricken silence, and kicked so hard as to almost jump from his hand. He looked at it in bewilderment. Something must be the matter with the gun—it had never kicked that way before.

But he saw that McAllister was running for the shelter of some rocks and then he broke into a shambling, uncertain run. "Stop and fight, you yellow skunk," Lance yelled, back behind his swollen throat and useless tongue.

McAllister stood up behind the rocks and began shouting something at him, and waving his hands. The sounds came only dimly through the pounding in his ears and the scarlet haze over his brain. He shot again and ran on.

The man ahead of him ducked down behind the rocks then, and Lance staggered toward him, weaving. He had him now, he thought exultingly—he had him, if only he could find the strength to raise that terribly heavy gun in his hand. He must have gotten somebody else's gun by mistake.

He had him—if only he could keep going forward and didn't lose sight of those rocks. They kept wavering away from him.

Then suddenly, he was close to them and McAllister, gun in hand, popped up from behind them. Lance jerked his gun upward with all his force, but the effort made him forget his feet and he stumbled as the Colt went off. But he never heard its roar—he had a vision of McAllister's strained face, of McAllister's gun leveled at him, and then something exploded in a blinding flash in the very center of his brain and the world went black....

CHAPTER 14
CRIMSON DAWN

DOC GRIMSON awakened wide-eyed and wholly conscious, in his usual cat-like fashion—not because anything had happened to disturb him, but because the alarm clock in his mind told him it was his time to wake up.

The first faint light of dawn was making pale, colorless oblongs of the firing slits. Within the room it was still dark, with a darkness somehow ameliorated, as a core of light had gotten within it. Doc made out the outline of Doris' head against one of the loopholes and went to her.

"Good morning," he said. "Everything quiet?"

"Good morning, Doc," she returned his greeting quietly. "Yes, everything is quiet. Too quiet, somehow."

In the gray light that came from the firing slit, her face looked colorless and weary, with great dark circles under the eyes. Doc tried to keep the shadow of worry out of his eyes as he answered lightly: "Oh, Lance will be along pretty soon. It's about time for him to get back."

In his heart, he knew that help had better come quickly, if it were to save this girl from complete collapse. She had been under enough strain to put any ordinary woman into a state of complete nervous disorganization. That night in Querida, which must have been terrifying for a girl who had been sheltered and gently reared; the terrific ordeal of the trip across the desert; and now this almost unbearable strain of fighting and waiting, of starving and going on short rations of water—all these were enough to try the strongest and healthiest. But in Doris' case, Doc felt, there was something more. She had been a changed girl since McAllister's brutal desertion. The spring had gone out of her carriage, the lift from her chin; the odd, delicate gallantry with which she had faced danger and hardship had given place to a strained impassivity, as though she were trying not to give way to a profound indifference as to what was to become of her and the men with her.

But Doc knew that you could be listless and indifferent to life and yet fear death. He knew that the uncertainty and strain of their long vigil was telling on her badly. And she was not sleeping. That was the worst symptom of all. It was for that reason, as well as to spare Flint and Charlie, that he let her stand guard. It gave her something definite to do and a necessary sense of her own usefulness.

"We don't even know that Lance got through," she told him, with a wry little smile which said plainly enough, "Why keep on trying to fool ourselves?"

"Oh, he got through all right," Doc said confidently. "These buzzards would have been around to show us his head if they had gotten him. And you can bet he's on his way back here with help right now. He'd cross that desert without food or water, just to get the best of McAllister, if for no other reason."

The girl's eyes filled suddenly with tears and her lips quivered.

Doc put his hand gently on her shoulder. "If you'd break down and cry about it," he said, "it'd be better for you. You went right on loving him, up to the very moment he pulled out on us, didn't you?"

"I've found out that you can't do anything about being in love," Doris said in a voice which shook a little. "You just aren't, or you just are—there doesn't seem to be any reason in it."

"Some reason," Doc amended gently. "He's a good deal of a man in a good many ways. I thought for a while that his badness was mostly bluff and that he'd turn out all right. But Doris, when they're really bad, then they're just bad—that's all. Nothin' ever changes 'em. He was in love with you, too, in his way. I could see that. If he was goin' to show himself a white man, that would have made him do it. If he missed that chance, then there's no hope. You had better think of him as dead. Cry over it, honey. Mourn him as much as you want to—there's no shame in having loved. But think of him as dead."

The girl covered her face with her hands and began to cry in low sobs that seemed to wrench all her slender body, but after a second she fought them back and faced Doc steadily. "I won't cry," she said. "I have my pride. It is shameful to have loved a man who would do what he has done."

Doc patted her shoulder. "Sorry," he said gruffly. "Better go get us a little breakfast. There's still a few beans. Take half the water to make coffee with. We'll save the rest, to get us through the day. All this will be over pretty soon."

He spoke with a confidence he didn't feel. He knew how little chance Lance had had of getting through the dangers which had beset him—knew how slender a thread their lives hung on. This was the last of the food and the water. Ammunition was getting low. They were already weakened by wounds and starvation and thirst. The end was not far away.

FLINT AND Charlie came awake and took their share of coffee and beans. They, too, spoke cheerfully of Lance's probable arrival with help that day. Doc smiled a little to himself with affection and admiration. They were worse off than anybody else, wounded as they were, and they knew as well as he what a slim hope they had, but you'd have thought they were discussing the arrival of the mail, which had been slightly delayed but was sure to come.

Doris brought him his coffee and beans to the loophole, so that he could eat while still standing guard.

A group of Yaquis had come out on the ridge a couple of hundred yards away. They drew to one side now, leaving a single figure isolated against the skyline. It was the figure of a big-shouldered, slender-hipped young man, dressed in American clothes.

Doris gasped. "It's Lance!" she cried, in a voice which was like a groan. "They got him!"

Flint and Charlie and Lockjaw crowded up to the slits. "It's him, all right," Lockjaw said excitedly. "That's his hat—sure! I'd know the shape of it anywheres."

"That's his shirt, too, I reckon," Flint said soberly.

Charlie Parr shook his head, frowning. "That ain't Lance," he growled finally.

"Why shore it's him, Charlie," Lockjaw told him earnestly. "That's his hat, ain't it? Why, Lance set a lot of store by that Stetson. Cost him a hundred dollars, it did. He wouldn't let nobody git that away from him."

Charlie looked stubborn. "It ain't Lance," he repeated.

"Why do you think that, Charlie?" Doris asked him, puzzled.

"I dunno," Charlie told her, "but it ain't Lance. Maybe he ain't tall enough or heavy enough through the shoulders, or somethin'. Them's his clothes, all right, but the man in 'em ain't Lance. There's just something about him that ain't—ain't *like*."

Doc said quietly: "That's the way it seems to me, Charlie. But it's hard to be sure at this distance."

He didn't want to admit completely that the bound figure before them was not Lance, because if it was not, that meant that Lance was dead!

The Yaquis were yelling now and gesturing toward the figure. Then in a moment an Indian with an air of authority stepped from the corner of the nearest building and held up his hand in a gesture of peace. He made a speech in Yaqui, which nobody understood. Doc replied in Spanish, telling him that they did not speak Yaqui.

The Indian said, in broken Spanish: "You surrender, we no kill your friend."

Doc said: "Do you take us for fools and children? That is not our friend."

"You think so?" the Yaqui replied boastfully. "We kill, then you know." But Doc thought there had been an instant of surprised hesitation before the answer.

He said: "Our friend is a great warrior. He would never let himself be taken by dogs like you. What have you done with him—killed him?"

The Yaqui spat angrily on the ground in front of him. "The white dog is a fool," he said. "Why does not Señor McAllister speak? He knows the tongue of the Yaquis."

"He is no longer here," Doc said. "He has escaped by a secret way and will bring help. Many soldiers are coming. You will all be killed."

The Indian looked sly. "He has perhaps been killed, eh?" he suggested. "You better give up. We kill your friend, then we kill you."

Doc did not answer at once. He looked at Charlie Parr. Charlie's eyes were agonized but his mouth was stubborn. "It's a trick," he insisted. "Even if it was Lance it wouldn't do no good to give ourselves up. They'd just kill us all."

"It's Lance's hat," Lockjaw insisted, equally stubborn. "Let's go out now and git him. Them Injuns ain't nothin' to fight."

Doc looked at Flint, whose eyes agreed fiercely with Lockjaw. There wasn't much chance that such a sortie would succeed, but if that *was* Lance out there....

The girl answered his thought by saying: "Don't think of me, Doc. If that is Lance, I want to go to help him, too."

Doc shook his head reluctantly. "They'd kill him before we got there," he said.

LOCKJAW BROKE in excitedly. "No they wouldn't, Doc. They're in range. If we all start shooting at once—sudden—we can pick off that crowd before they hurt him, then we can make a break for him. They'll be too busy takin' care of themselves to bother him."

Charlie Parr said: "I'll go if you fellers want to—but that ain't Lance. Look at the way he keeps his head down. Lance'd be tryin' to make us signs with his head."

That decided Doc. He had a strong hunch that Charlie was

right, and he was too much of a gambler not to play his hunch. If they got drawn out by a trick, none of them might get back. He shook his head. "Charlie's right," he said. "We'd just fall into a trap."

Lockjaw looked sulky. "Aw, shucks," he said, and it was plain that if it had been anybody but Doc and Charlie he would have rebelled.

But Flint did his rebelling for him. "Look here, Doc," he said. "You know I've never been against you before—you've been the boss as far as I'm concerned. But this is different. I don't know if that's Lance out there or not. But, listen, if it was an' we didn't go to him, there wouldn't be one of us could look each other in the face or live with ourselves the rest of our lives. You can stay if you want to, but me—I got to try to get to Lance!"

Lockjaw's dumb, horse-like, wooden face lit up like a child's. "That's shoutin' a mouthful, Flint," he cried. "Deal me in, feller— we'll show these here lemon-colored skunks who to fool with!"

Almost at once, he was overcome with his own temerity. He turned apologetically to Doc and Charlie. "I shore hope you'll excuse me, Charlie—I shore hope you and Doc will," he said pleadingly. "But that there's Lance's hat and Lance'd shore be under it. I got to go with Flint."

Doc Grimson looked at Flint Maddox with eyes that were suddenly softer than anybody had yet seen them. "You got a leg you can't run on, haven't you, you mule-headed horsethief?" he said. "But you're goin' to run on it anyway, aren't you? You're goin' to use it to run up to Boot Hill with. Because you think

Lance may be out there needin' you. Well, I'm runnin' with you, feller. Lead the way—you're boss here now!"

Charlie Parr spoke like a man with a grievance, but his voice was husky. "I reckon I'll have to play along," he growled. "It's what comes of trailin' with a lot of danged fools!"

Doris Enderby cried: "I'm glad. I'm going too. I can shoot. Lance would do the same for us."

Flint turned away to hide the workings of his face. "Let's begin with the rifles like Lockjaw said," he got out, gruffly.

From outside came the voice of the Yaqui. "Well? We no wait longer."

"Just give us a minute. We're talking it over," Doc called to him.

"You better hurry!" The Indian's voice had the beginning of triumph in it.

They lined up at the firing slits. "There are eight of them," Flint said. "Pick the nearest Lance, in order. Then the other four. Be sure to keep your muzzles from showing outside the slits."

He sighted carefully and then said: *"Now!"*

The four rifles spoke almost as one. Four Yaquis went down, clawing the air, clutching their bodies, tumbling, some sideways, some forward—as some invisible blight had struck them. The others stood a fatal second, paralyzed. They had expected that the white men in the adobe would be afraid to fire on them because they would believe their friend would be killed. They stood, not quite long enough for the four Mavericks to lever and aim again, then they broke and ran. Two more of them dropped.

And then the four men and girl were at the door, were outside, running toward the bound figure which now lay prone on the ground, having thrown himself down after the first volley. Four men and a girl—eight six-guns and a rifle blazing unexpected death.

The suddenness and fierceness of the attack took the Yaquis by surprise and the five had traversed half the distance toward their objective before any considerable firing began to answer them. Indians came running then, from the camp streets, from the ground behind the ridge, from positions behind the adobe, from every side. And at that moment, when the certainty of disaster began to close in on them, the prone figure on the ridge raised its head, showed a terrified face—the face, not of Lance Clayton but of a Yaqui Indian!

"To the rocks!" Doc Grimson yelled, "to the rocks on the right!" They were trapped—and for nothing!

IT WAS the only shelter available. They ran for them, took what cover they afforded—which was not very much.

"Sorry, Doc," Flint gasped.

Doc said warmly: "Forget it! You did the right thing. I was hopin' you would."

Flint looked his gratitude for that but there wasn't time for any more talk. The Yaquis were closing in from all sides, firing as they came. It was a question now of selling their lives as dearly as possible—nothing more. And the price would be paid, the bargain concluded, within a very few minutes.

So occupied were they with the mere business of hurling hot lead into that oncoming, encircling mob that they scarcely heard the sudden, urgent shouts of several Indians near the adobe. Then Charlie Parr, who was facing in that direction, gave a sudden, unbelieving exclamation.

Up the slope behind the adobe charged a solitary rider, spurring a lathered horse in a dead run. It was clear that by now, he must see the number and force of the Yaquis—must see that he was about to commit suicide—but nonetheless he came on. His face was so covered with dust and sweat as to be almost unrecognizable, and he was yelling like a fiend out of hell, riding without his reins, his two guns beating a staccato accompaniment to the racing beat of the horse's hoofs.

"By God!" Charlie Parr marvelled, his tone still unbelieving. "It's McAllister!"

The Yaquis, startled by this sudden apparition and its inexplicable charge into the arms of what seemed certain death, had momentarily ceased firing. Now, however, as he came racing almost to the muzzles of the guns, a great blast of lead sung toward the riding figure. The gray dust leaped from his clothes in half a dozen places. He reeled in the saddle, toppled, and fell heavily to the ground.

And then, up the slope behind him, swept other mounted figures—a dozen, twenty—half a hundred—and ahead of them, spurring a jaded mount into a final desperate spurt, rode Lance Clayton.

The Yaquis let out yells of terror at the sight, for these men, riding with the careless grace of born horsemen and the cruel joy of battle on their faces were the most feared men in Mexico—the Rurales!

Lance Clayton hit the dirt beside his friends, but the rest of the troup swept on after the Indians, shooting them down.

"Nobody hurt bad?" Lance asked.

"Nobody but McAllister," Doc told him briefly. "Glad to see you, boy. You just about hit it in time." As he spoke he was already moving toward the limp figure of the superintendent. But Doris Enderby was ahead of him.

She flung herself down beside McAllister, crying, "Bart! Bart! Are you hurt? Don't die, Bart; don't die, darling—"

Lance said: "He was goin' for help all the time—slipped out so none of us would try to face the trip. I tried to kill him in the desert—he was shootin' to disable me when I stumbled and took it in the head—just a crease, but enough to knock me out. He brought me in."

Charlie Parr said: "I reckon we all owe him a sort of apology."

"He's all man," Lance agreed.

Lockjaw broke in in a bewildered tone: "How come you let the Injuns have your hat, Lance?"

Lance looked surprised. "Oh!" he said, "I guess I went sort of loco and threw it away in the desert. The Yaquis must have come up later and picked it up. How'd you happen to see, and how come you was out of the fort?"

Charlie Parr grinned. "We come out to get it. Lockjaw and Flint was kind of sore because the Injuns was wearin' it," he explained. "Lockjaw said it was worth a hundred dollars and too good for an Injun."

Doc Grimson looked up from his examination of McAllister. "He's hit in several places but only one of them is really bad," he said to the girl. "I think he'll pull through all right."

McAllister opened his eyes. "Hell, yes," he said faintly, "I—got something—to pull through—for—*now.*" He looked at Doris and his lips parted in a feeble smile.

Doris Enderby broke down and cried then. "Oh," she sobbed, "Oh, Bart—*darling!*" And then she couldn't say any more for the sobs which racked her.

Lockjaw shook his head, with a look of mild, philosophic astonishment on his face. "Women," he announced in a wondering voice, "women is shore funny!"

www.ingramcontent.com/pod-product-compliance
Lightning Source LLC
Chambersburg PA
CBHW071944170626
46813CB00005B/1827